# Also by Rachael Reed

**Sis**
Sis 2 Blood on the Streets

**Standalone**
Codefendant
Codefendant
Once a Cheater
Once a Cheater
Passport Bro
What Happens in Prison
Preference
Sprinkle Sprinkle
Championship Bad
Street Exodus
Street Exodus
Street Royalty
Pawns of Power
SIS
Cartel Bloodline
Get Money Girls
Skip the Games
Til Death Do Us Part

Backpage Hustle
Link in Bio
The Virgin and The Kingpin
A Gangsta's Heart
Boosters
Can't Turn a Hoe Into a Housewife
Better you Than Me
Wig Dealer: How to Start Your wig Business
Trail Ride Blues
Demure Diva
Queen of the Carnival
Caribbean Carnival Hoe
How to Glow Up! Make 2025 Your Best Year
How to Lose 10 Pounds in a Month
What is Project 2025? The Easy to Understand Guide
What Is A Tariff
Natural Hair Growth Oil with 50 Recipes
Regrow Hair Naturally in 3 Weeks
Hustlin Through the Holidays
Same Shit Different Year
Return to Sender
85 South
Everybody That Grin Ain't Ya Friend

# Everybody That Grin Ain't Ya Friend

Everybody That Grin Ain't Ya Friend

By TBDB PUBLISHING

# Chapter 1: Welcome to My World

The sound of laughter and loud conversation filled the corner café where Brittany held conversation, her vibrant energy commanding the space like a spotlight. Her voice was warm and melodic, laced with the kind of sass and confidence that made you want to be her friend or, at the very least, stand close enough to catch some of her glow.

"Girl, I told him straight up, 'If you ain't gon' pay these bills, then don't worry 'bout how I'm gettin' 'em paid,'" Brittany said, flipping her hair over her shoulder as her girls howled with laughter.

Her world was tight-knit people came to her for advice, drama, or just to bask in the good vibes she radiated. She wasn't the type to deal in mess, but somehow, she was always in the mix. Her best friend, Tanisha, leaned across the table, waving her manicured hand.

"Britt, you too damn bold. That's why folks scared to cross you," Tanisha said with a smirk.

"And that's why they stay in line," Brittany shot back with a wink. Her honey-brown skin glistened under the dim café lights, her hoop earrings swinging with every exaggerated gesture. Brittany didn't just light up a room she owned it.

But that night, the usual rhythm of her life would change.

The bell over the café door jingled, and Brittany glanced up out of habit. A slim woman stepped inside, moving like she didn't want to take up too much space. Her clothes were plain washed-out jeans and a hoodie that looked two sizes too big but her wide eyes and shy smile caught Brittany's attention.

"Who that?" Brittany murmured to Tanisha, her tone curious but cautious.

"Don't know. She look like she lost or somethin'," Tanisha replied, her voice tinged with disinterest.

The woman hesitated by the door, scanning the room like she wasn't sure where she belonged. Brittany felt a pang of something pity, maybe? Nah, she didn't do pity. Compassion, maybe. Whatever it was, it made her wave the girl over.

"Hey, you lookin' for somebody?" Brittany called, her tone friendly but firm.

The woman blinked, then shuffled forward, clutching a small purse to her chest. "Um, no... I just moved here. Thought I'd check this place out. I'm Gloria."

Her voice was soft, barely audible over the chatter in the café. Brittany tilted her head, studying her. Something about the girl seemed off not in a bad way, just... different.

"Well, welcome to the neighborhood, Gloria," Brittany said, her smile genuine. "Come sit with us. We don't bite... much."

Tanisha raised an eyebrow, clearly unimpressed, but didn't say anything. Brittany scooted over, making room at the table. Gloria sat gingerly, like she wasn't sure if she was invited to stay long.

"So, where you from?" Brittany asked, leaning in like she was genuinely interested.

"Up north," Gloria said vaguely, her eyes darting around the table.

"Up north where?" Tanisha pressed, her voice sharper than necessary.

"Ohio," Gloria mumbled, looking down at her hands.

Brittany shot Tanisha a look, silently telling her to chill. "Ohio, huh? Bet it's cold as hell up there."

Gloria smiled faintly, her eyes flicking up to meet Brittany's. "Yeah. This is a nice change."

"Well, you in the right spot now," Brittany said, her tone light. "Atlanta gon' show you some things if you let it."

Gloria nodded, her smile growing. "Thanks. I... I really needed this."

The next few days flew by, with Brittany taking Gloria under her wing like she'd been a part of the crew forever. It wasn't unusual for Brittany to play mentor to someone new it was just who she was. But Gloria? She was different. Quiet, almost too quiet. She didn't ask for much, didn't say much either, but she soaked up everything Brittany showed her like a sponge.

"Girl, you gotta loosen up," Brittany said one night as they got ready to hit the club. Gloria had been trying to decide between two outfits for the past twenty minutes, her face twisted in concentration.

"I just... I don't wanna look stupid," Gloria said, her voice barely above a whisper.

"Ain't nobody gon' think you look stupid," Brittany said, rolling her eyes. "Now put that little black dress on and let's go."

When Gloria finally emerged, dressed in the outfit Brittany picked out, something shifted. The shy girl from Ohio looked like she belonged her hair slicked back, her makeup subtle but flawless. For a moment, Brittany felt a flicker of pride, like she'd created something new.

"You look good," Brittany said with a grin. "Now don't embarrass me in this club."

At the club, Brittany introduced Gloria to everyone her circle, her co-workers, even Marcus, her boyfriend. Gloria smiled and nodded, her eyes wide as she took it all in. She barely spoke, but her presence was felt. She had a way of blending into the background while still being noticed.

"You got a cool vibe," Marcus said later that night as they walked to the car. "She quiet, but she cool."

"Right?" Brittany said, her tone light. "I think she just needs some time to settle in. Atlanta can be a lot."

Marcus nodded, but something in his expression gave Brittany pause. It wasn't anything obvious, just a flicker of... interest? Curiosity? She shook it off, telling herself she was overthinking.

As the weeks passed, Gloria became a fixture in Brittany's world. She showed up at events, joined the group chats, even started working at the same spot as Brittany. At first, it felt natural like she was just finding her place. But slowly, things started to feel... off.

Brittany couldn't put her finger on it, but something about Gloria's energy began to shift. She started dressing like Brittany, talking like her, even mimicking her little quirks. At first, Brittany laughed it off.

"Girl, you tryna be me or somethin'?" she joked one day.

Gloria froze for a moment, then smiled. "You're just... inspiring, that's all."

Brittany laughed, but the comment lingered in her mind.

One night, Brittany came home to find Gloria sitting on her porch. She frowned, her keys in hand. "What you doin' here?"

"I just... I wanted to talk," Gloria said, her voice small. "I didn't know where else to go."

Brittany sighed, unlocking the door. "Alright, come on in."

They sat on the couch, Gloria fidgeting with the hem of her shirt. "I just... I feel like I don't belong anywhere," she said, her voice trembling. "But you... you make me feel like I do."

Brittany felt a pang of sympathy, but something about the way Gloria said it made her uncomfortable. "Look, you belong here, aight? You ain't gotta try so hard. Just be you."

Gloria nodded, her eyes glistening. "Thanks, Brittany. You're... you're everything I want to be."

As Brittany closed the door after Gloria left, a chill ran down her spine. She shook her head, trying to brush it off. But deep down, she knew something wasn't right.

And for the first time, she wondered if bringing Gloria into her world was the biggest mistake she'd ever made.

# Chapter 2: New Friend

The salon was buzzing that Saturday morning, the sound of flat irons sizzling and women talking louder than the music blasting through the speakers. Brittany sat in her usual chair, scrolling through her phone while Tanisha got her weave tightened up. The two of them came here like clockwork every other week, a ritual they'd started years ago. It was their space, their vibe.

"Yo, Britt," Tanisha said, glancing up from her phone. "Ain't that your girl Gloria?"

Brittany followed Tanisha's gaze to the door, and there she was Gloria, standing awkwardly near the counter. She wore skinny jeans, a cropped jacket, and gold hoops that looked suspiciously like the pair Brittany had worn last week.

"Girl, what she doin' here?" Tanisha asked, raising an eyebrow.

Brittany shrugged, though her stomach flipped. "She probably just tryna find a spot to get her hair done. Ain't no big deal."

But as Gloria made her way toward them, a wide smile on her face, Brittany felt something shift. This wasn't a coincidence.

"Hey, Britt!" Gloria said, her voice chipper. "Didn't know you'd be here!"

Brittany forced a smile. "Yeah, I come here all the time. What's up?"

"Oh, I just... thought I'd check this place out. You know, needed a new spot."

"Right," Tanisha muttered under her breath, but Brittany shot her a warning glance.

"Well, you in the right place," Brittany said, keeping her tone light. "They'll hook you up."

That should've been it, but it wasn't. Over the next week, Gloria started showing up everywhere Brittany went her favorite café, the gym, even the boutique she hit up for outfits. At first, Brittany laughed it off.

"Girl, we keep bumpin' into each other," she said during one of their accidental meetings.

"I know, right?" Gloria replied with that same wide-eyed smile. "I guess we got the same taste."

But by the third time, it wasn't funny anymore. Brittany couldn't shake the feeling that Gloria was keeping tabs on her, tracking her moves. And then there were the comments from her friends.

"Yo, is it just me, or Gloria tryna dress like you?" Tanisha asked one afternoon while they were getting ready for a brunch.

Brittany laughed it off, though it gnawed at her. "She just admirin' my style, T. Let the girl live."

"Admire is one thing. Copyin' is somethin' else," Tanisha shot back, but Brittany waved her off.

The brunch was supposed to be a small, private thing just Brittany and her close friends catching up over mimosas and pancakes. So when Gloria strolled in halfway through, dressed in a dress nearly identical to Brittany's, the table went silent.

"Hey, y'all!" Gloria chirped, pulling up a chair like she'd been invited.

Brittany's smile froze. "Gloria? How you know 'bout this?"

"Oh, I saw it on Instagram," Gloria said casually, pouring herself a drink from the pitcher in the middle of the table. "Figured it'd be fun to join."

Tanisha's side-eye could've cut glass. "That's bold as hell," she muttered under her breath, loud enough for Brittany to hear.

Brittany cleared her throat, trying to play it cool. "Well, uh, welcome, I guess."

The rest of the brunch was tense. Gloria laughed too loud, chimed in on stories she had no business knowing, and even offered to pick up the tab a move that left the rest of the group side-eyeing her even harder. By the time it was over, Brittany's nerves were frayed.

"Britt, we gotta talk," Tanisha said later as they walked to their cars. "Yo, that girl is doin' the most. Showin' up uninvited, actin' like she runnin' shit? Nah, somethin' ain't right."

Brittany sighed, rubbing her temples. "I know, T. But what I'm supposed to do? Tell her she can't be friends with me?"

"Friends? That girl ain't your friend. She tryna *be* you," Tanisha said, her tone serious. "You better keep your eyes open, Britt. I'm tellin' you."

Brittany waved her off again, but Tanisha's words stuck with her.

The next few weeks were more of the same. Gloria started popping up at Brittany's job, bringing coffee for her and the team like she was part of the crew. Brittany's co-workers started noticing, too.

"Yo, Britt, your girl Gloria cool, but... she don't know boundaries, huh?" one of them joked one afternoon.

"Yeah, it's... she just real friendly," Brittany replied, forcing a laugh.

But deep down, she felt the unease growing.

One night, Brittany and Marcus were out at their favorite spot, enjoying a date night. The music was loud, the drinks flowing, and for once, Brittany felt like she could breathe. That is, until she spotted Gloria across the room, leaning against the bar.

"Yo, ain't that your homegirl?" Marcus asked, nodding toward her.

Brittany froze. "What the hell she doin' here?"

Gloria spotted them a second later and lit up like a Christmas tree. She weaved through the crowd, her smile wide as ever. "Hey, Britt! Marcus! Fancy seein' y'all here."

Marcus gave her a polite nod, but Brittany's jaw tightened. "Hey, Gloria. You out with somebody?"

"Nope, just me," Gloria said cheerfully. "Figured I'd check this place out. Heard you talk about it before."

Brittany forced a smile, but her blood boiled. This was her spot her and Marcus's. And Gloria had inserted herself here, too.

By the time they got home that night, Brittany couldn't hold it in anymore.

"Marcus, don't you think it's weird?" she asked, pacing the living room. "She just... she everywhere. All the time."

Marcus leaned back on the couch, his expression calm. "I mean, yeah, it's a little much. But maybe she just lookin' for friends. You said she new in town."

"But it ain't just that," Brittany snapped. "She dressin' like me, talkin' like me. She even showed up to brunch uninvited."

Marcus shrugged. "Maybe she just look up to you. You know you got that kinda energy."

Brittany sighed, flopping onto the couch beside him. "I don't know, Marcus. Somethin' don't feel right."

He wrapped an arm around her, pulling her close. "Don't stress it, Britt. I'm sure its really nothing."

But Brittany couldn't shake the feeling. Gloria was worming her way deeper into her life, and no matter how much Brittany tried to brush it off, the unease gnawed at her. Every time she saw Gloria's face, that same too-wide smile, her stomach churned.

And then one night, she got a text.

*"You're so amazing, Britt. I just wanna thank you for everything. I hope I can be just like you one day."*

Brittany stared at the message, her fingers trembling. For the first time, she wasn't flattered. She was scared.

# Chapter 3: The Perfect Copy

The late afternoon sun poured into Brittany's apartment as she flopped onto the couch, scrolling aimlessly through Instagram. Her nails were freshly done a bold red with rhinestones that sparkled under the light. She had just posted a selfie that was already racking up likes. Marcus was in the kitchen, humming some old-school R&B while fixing them drinks. It should've been a perfect vibe, but something was eating at her.

Scrolling through her feed, she froze. There it was. A new post from Gloria.

The photo hit Brittany like a punch to the gut. Gloria was rocking the same exact hairstyle Brittany had posted about last week. Braids with gold cuffs, slicked edges, and even the same color tips. The caption read: *"Feelin' myself today ◇◇ Thanks to @HairByKeisha for slayin' me!"*

Brittany's stomach twisted. *HairByKeisha* was *her* stylist. Brittany had sent Gloria to her once and now here she was, practically stealing her whole look.

"Yo, Marcus," Brittany called, holding up her phone. "Come look at this."

Marcus strolled over, two glasses in hand, and peered at the screen. "Damn, she look just like you," he said with a chuckle. "You got yourself a lil' twin now."

Brittany frowned, her chest tightening. "This shit ain't funny, Marcus. She even tagged my stylist. Like, who does that?"

He shrugged, setting the drinks down. "Maybe she just admires you, Britt. You know you got that influence. People be tryna follow your lead."

"Yeah, but this different," Brittany muttered, scrolling through more of Gloria's posts. There it was again Gloria wearing a jumpsuit almost identical to one Brittany had rocked at brunch last month. Another post showed Gloria at the same yoga studio Brittany had been raving about.

Marcus kissed her forehead and picked up his drink. "You overthinkin' it, babe. Take it as a compliment. You the blueprint."

But Brittany wasn't so sure.

The next time Brittany saw Gloria, it was at the weekly girls' night. Tanisha had organized it, and Brittany had almost skipped out, but something told her to show up. When she walked into the bar, her eyes immediately landed on Gloria.

Her breath caught in her throat.

Gloria was wearing *the dress*. Not just any dress, but Brittany's signature red bodycon dress the one she wore on her birthday last year and had posted all over her socials. Gloria had even paired it with gold hoops and the same heels Brittany owned.

"Yo, Britt," Tanisha hissed, grabbing her arm. "What the hell is goin' on? Why she out here lookin' like your clone?"

"I don't know," Brittany said through gritted teeth, forcing a smile as she approached the table. "Hey, y'all."

"Brittany!" Gloria beamed, standing up to hug her. "You look so good! We twinning tonight, huh?"

Brittany's smile faltered. "Yeah... somethin' like that."

Tanisha shot Brittany a look, her eyebrows raised so high they almost touched her hairline. "Twinning" didn't even begin to cover it.

As the night went on, Gloria took over the conversation. She laughed louder than anyone, chimed in with stories that didn't even make sense, and kept leaning into Brittany's space like she was trying to merge into her body.

"Girl, I been hittin' that yoga studio you told me about," Gloria said, turning to Brittany. "It's so peaceful, ain't it?"

Brittany nodded, her unease growing. "Yeah, it's cool. Been goin' there for years."

"Oh, me too now," Gloria said with a bright smile. "Maybe we should go together sometime."

Tanisha leaned over, her voice low. "Yo, she buggin'. This some Single White Female type shit."

"Chill," Brittany whispered back, though her stomach churned.

But the breaking point came when Gloria brought up Marcus.

"You so lucky, Britt," Gloria said, swirling her drink. "Marcus is such a good guy. Y'all really inspire me, you know? Like, that's the kind of love I want."

Brittany's jaw clenched. The way Gloria said it felt too personal, too familiar. She glanced at Tanisha, who looked like she was ready to explode.

"Girl, you talkin' like you know Marcus or somethin'," Tanisha said, her tone sharp. "You met him like, what, once?"

Gloria's smile faltered for a split second before she recovered. "I just mean... he seems like the real deal. That's rare."

Brittany forced a laugh, but inside, her unease grew. Gloria wasn't just mimicking her style she was sliding into every part of her life.

The next day, Brittany was at home scrolling through her phone when a notification popped up. Gloria had tagged her in a post. With a heavy sigh, she opened it.

It was a picture of Gloria holding a Starbucks cup with "Brittany" written on it in marker. The caption read: *"Guess they thought I was Brittany today 👯‍♀️😁 Twins for real!"*

Brittany stared at the screen, her heart racing. It wasn't cute. It wasn't funny. It was creepy.

Before she could overthink it, she dialed Tanisha.

"Yo, T," Brittany said when she picked up. "This girl Gloria... I think she tryna take my whole life."

"Bitch, I been told you that," Tanisha snapped. "What she do now?"

Brittany explained the post, her words tumbling out in frustration. "It's like... she watchin' me, T. Like she studyin' me or some shit."

Tanisha was quiet for a moment. "You gotta cut her off, Britt. Like, now. Before this shit go too far."

"But how?" Brittany asked, her voice trembling. "She everywhere. And what if I'm wrong?"

"You ain't wrong," Tanisha said firmly. "Trust your gut. That girl ain't right."

That evening, Marcus came over, and Brittany tried to bring it up.

"Marcus, you ever think Gloria act... weird?" she asked as they sat on the couch.

"Weird how?" he asked, sipping his beer.

"Like... she copyin' me. The way she talk, dress, even where she go. It's like she tryna be me."

Marcus chuckled, shaking his head. "Britt, you overthinking. She just look up to you. Ain't nothin' wrong with that."

"But it don't feel right," Brittany insisted. "It's too much."

Marcus kissed her forehead, his voice soft. "You got a good heart, babe. Don't let this girl mess with your head."

Brittany sighed, leaning into him. Maybe he was right. Maybe she was just overreacting.

But deep down, she knew better.

As Brittany lay in bed that night, she couldn't shake the feeling of unease. She grabbed her phone and scrolled through Gloria's Instagram again, looking for clues. Post after post mirrored her own life, her own style.

And then she saw it.

A picture of Gloria standing in front of a mural Brittany had posted weeks ago. The caption read: *"This spot is so me* ☺ *Thanks for the inspo, @BrittanyBee!"*

Brittany's heart pounded. This wasn't admiration. This was obsession.

She closed her eyes, trying to calm her racing thoughts. But one thing was clear: Gloria wasn't just a new friend. She was something much darker.

# Chapter 4: A Sudden Shift

The air felt thick in the cramped lounge where Brittany and her crew were hanging out. It was supposed to be a chill night just drinks, laughs, and catching up. But the vibe was off. Real off. Brittany couldn't put her finger on it, but the tension was like a rope tightening around her chest.

Gloria, of course, was front and center, her presence impossible to ignore. She was louder tonight, bolder, throwing her two cents into every conversation like she'd been part of the crew for years. Brittany shifted in her seat, watching as Gloria's hands gestured wildly, her laugh cutting through the room like a knife.

"So I told dude straight up," Gloria said, her voice carrying over the low hum of the music, "if you ain't bringin' nothin' to the table, then why you even sittin' at it?"

The group chuckled, but Brittany's stomach twisted. That was *her* line something she'd said just last week. Gloria said it with the same cadence, the same energy, like it was hers to begin with.

"Yo, Britt," Tanisha said, leaning in close. "You peepin' this?"

Brittany nodded, her jaw tight. She had peeped it. She'd been peeping it for weeks. But what was she supposed to do? Start an argument in front of everybody?

As the night went on, Gloria's behavior escalated. She interrupted Brittany mid-story about a work win, cutting her off with a dismissive laugh. "Oh, girl, you always makin' shit sound bigger than it is," Gloria said, her tone playful but laced with something sharper. "It's just a lil' job promotion. Ain't like you CEO or somethin.'"

The room went quiet for a beat, the group exchanging awkward glances. Brittany's chest burned, but she forced a smile. "Yeah, well, it's still a big deal to me."

"Of course it is," Gloria said, flashing that same too-wide grin. "I'm just sayin'... keepin' it real."

Tanisha shifted uncomfortably in her seat, giving Brittany a look that said *Don't let her get away with that.* But Brittany swallowed her anger, not wanting to make a scene. Not yet.

The cracks in her friendships started small but noticeable. One by one, her friends seemed a little more distant, a little less involved. Tanisha was still riding for her, but even she was getting sucked into Gloria's charm.

"Gloria been hittin' me up lately," Tanisha mentioned one afternoon. "She real cool once you get to know her."

Brittany raised an eyebrow. "She hittin' you up? For what?"

"Just, like, talkin' and stuff. She said she don't got many friends, so I been tryin' to be nice."

Brittany bit her tongue, her frustration bubbling beneath the surface. It wasn't just Tanisha. Gloria had been sliding into everyone's space texting them, meeting them for coffee, even planning little hangouts without Brittany. And nobody seemed to think it was weird.

One night, Brittany got a text from her friend Kelly. *"Yo, you comin' to the thing at Gloria's tomorrow?"*

Brittany frowned, rereading the message. *What thing?*

*"She said it's a lil' game night. Didn't she invite you?"*

Brittany stared at her phone, her fingers trembling. Game night? Gloria hadn't said a word to her about it. She felt her chest tighten, the realization hitting her like a punch: Gloria was trying to edge her out of her own circle.

By the time she confronted Gloria, the girl had perfected the art of gaslighting. It was a Sunday afternoon, and they were sitting in Brittany's living room, Gloria perched on the edge of the couch like she didn't have a care in the world.

"Yo, Gloria," Brittany started, her voice steady but firm. "I been noticin' some things."

"Like what?" Gloria asked, tilting her head innocently.

"Like how you always tryna step in and take over," Brittany said, crossing her arms. "You showin' up uninvited, tryna slide into my friendships, even plannin' stuff behind my back. What's up with that?"

Gloria's face fell, her wide eyes filling with mock hurt. "Britt, what are you talkin' about? I thought we was cool. I didn't know I needed permission to hang out with people."

"It ain't about permission," Brittany snapped. "It's about respect."

Gloria shook her head, letting out a soft laugh. "Wow. I didn't know you felt like this. I'm just tryna fit in, and now you makin' me feel like I'm doin' somethin' wrong. That's crazy."

Brittany's jaw tightened. She knew what Gloria was doing flipping the script, making herself the victim. It was infuriating, but what could she say? Gloria's performance was flawless.

The final straw came at a party Brittany and Marcus hosted. It was supposed to be a casual get-together, just their closest friends. But Gloria, of course, found a way to make it about her.

She arrived late, her outfit almost identical to Brittany's a tight black dress with gold accessories. Marcus noticed immediately, his eyebrows shooting up. "Damn, y'all really do look like twins tonight," he joked, earning a glare from Brittany.

Throughout the night, Gloria monopolized every conversation, cutting Brittany off and redirecting the attention to herself. At one point, she even cornered Marcus in the kitchen, laughing too loudly at whatever he was saying.

Brittany watched from across the room, her blood boiling. She felt like a stranger in her own home, her life slipping out of her control.

Later that night, after the guests had left, Brittany sat on the couch, her head in her hands. Marcus sat beside her, rubbing her back.

"You good, babe?" he asked, his voice soft.

"No, I'm not good," she snapped, looking up at him. "Did you see how she was actin'? Like she runnin' shit?"

Marcus sighed, leaning back. "Britt, you overthinkin' again. Gloria's just tryna fit in. She don't mean no harm."

Brittany stared at him, her frustration boiling over. "Why you always takin' her side? You don't see how she tryna take over my life?"

"Ain't nobody takin' over your life," Marcus said, shaking his head. "You gotta chill."

Brittany stood up, pacing the room. She felt trapped, like nobody believed her, like Gloria had already won.

That night, Brittany lay awake, staring at the ceiling. The anger, the frustration, the helplessness all churned inside her like a storm. She didn't know what Gloria's endgame was, but one thing was clear: this wasn't admiration. This was an obsession.

# Chapter 5: Friends Turned Foes

Brittany sat at her vanity, staring at her reflection like it might give her some answers. Her honey-brown skin looked duller, her eyes tired. The usual spark she carried, the one people gravitated to, felt like it had dimmed. Everything about her world was off-kilter, and no matter how hard she tried, she couldn't shake the weight pressing down on her chest.

Her phone buzzed on the counter. She glanced at the screen: a text from Kelly.

*"Yo, Britt, you good? Heard you been actin' funny lately."*

Brittany frowned, her stomach twisting. *Funny?* What the hell was Kelly talking about? She typed back quickly: *"What you mean funny?"*

The three dots appeared, then disappeared. No reply.

Her hand clenched the phone, the frustration bubbling up. This wasn't the first time she'd gotten a message like that. Over the past week, the vibe with her crew had shifted hard. People weren't hitting her up like they used to. Conversations felt clipped, tense. And whenever Gloria was around, they seemed to orbit her like she was the sun.

"Girl, I'm tellin' you," Tanisha said, leaning across the table later that day. They'd met up at a diner on the west side, one of their usual spots. "Gloria been runnin' her mouth. I heard her talkin' to Kelly and Yolanda last night at the lounge."

"What she say?" Brittany asked, though she already knew it wouldn't be good.

Tanisha hesitated, glancing around before lowering her voice. "She said you jealous of her. That you don't like sharin' the spotlight and be tryna control people."

Brittany's jaw dropped. "What? Jealous of *her*? She tryna take my whole life!"

"I know, Britt," Tanisha said, her tone softening. "But you know how folks be. She real slick with it, sayin' it like she all innocent and shit. And now Kelly and Yolanda eatin' it up."

Brittany's stomach churned. "So they really out here believin' her? After all I done for them?"

Tanisha shrugged, sipping her lemonade. "I'm just lettin' you know what it is. You gotta watch what's goin on."

That night, Brittany decided to call Kelly. She couldn't let this slide.

"Hey, Kel," she said when her friend picked up. "We need to talk."

"What's up?" Kelly sounded distracted, her tone cooler than usual.

"I been hearin' some things," Brittany said, trying to keep her voice steady. "About Gloria sayin' I'm jealous or whatever. I just wanna know if you really believe that."

Kelly sighed. "Britt, look, I ain't tryin' to get in the middle of no drama. But you been actin' different lately. Like, I don't know... distant."

"Distant? How?" Brittany snapped. "I'm the one who's been gettin' iced out by y'all!"

Kelly paused, her silence saying more than words ever could. "I'm just sayin', Britt. Maybe you should talk to Gloria. Work it out."

Brittany gritted her teeth. "Gloria ain't the one who's been loyal to y'all for years. I am."

"Okay, but it don't gotta be like this," Kelly said, her voice defensive. "You makin' it a bigger deal than it is."

The call ended abruptly, leaving Brittany staring at her phone, her hands shaking. She felt like she was being swallowed whole, her world crumbling faster than she could hold it together.

The final blow came at a house party the following weekend. Marcus convinced her to go, saying it might help clear the air. Brittany wasn't sure, but she needed to show up, to remind people who she was.

The music was loud, the air thick with smoke and laughter. Brittany moved through the crowd, plastering a smile on her face, but the energy was all wrong. People gave her tight smiles, quick nods, then moved on like she wasn't worth stopping for.

And there was Gloria, standing in the kitchen, holding court. She was laughing, her voice cutting through the chatter, and Brittany's blood boiled as she watched her.

"Yo, Britt, glad you came," Marcus said, wrapping an arm around her. "You good?"

Brittany forced a smile. "Yeah. Just tryin' to figure out why people actin' brand new."

Marcus sighed, pulling her closer. "Don't let it get to you, babe. Just chill."

But chilling wasn't an option when she heard Gloria's voice cut through the room. "I mean, I get it. Some people just don't know how to handle not bein' the center of attention."

Laughter erupted, and Brittany's heart dropped. She knew who that was aimed at.

Brittany stormed into the kitchen, her fists clenched. "Yo, Gloria, we need to talk."

The room went silent, all eyes snapping to them. Gloria raised an eyebrow, feigning innocence. "What's up, Britt?"

"You know what's up," Brittany snapped. "You out here runnin' your mouth, turnin' people against me. You got somethin' to say? Say it to my face."

Gloria tilted her head, her lips curling into a smirk. "I don't know what you talkin' about. But if you feel some type of way, that's on you."

Brittany stepped closer, her voice low but fierce. "Nah, don't play dumb. You been tryna steal my entire life, my friends. And I'm done stayin' quiet."

"Steal your life?" Gloria laughed, the sound cold and sharp. "Britt, you trippin'. Maybe if you wasn't so insecure, you wouldn't be worried about me."

The words hit Brittany like a slap, but before she could respond, Marcus stepped between them. "Aight, that's enough," he said, his tone firm. "This ain't the place for all that."

Brittany stared at him, her chest heaving. "You really takin' her side?"

"I ain't takin' nobody's side," Marcus said, his voice low. "I'm just sayin', this ain't it."

The room buzzed with whispers, the tension thick enough to cut with a knife. Brittany turned on her heel, storming out of the party, tears stinging her eyes.

Back at home, Brittany sat on the edge of her bed, her hands trembling. She felt like she was drowning, her once-perfect life slipping through her fingers. Her friends, her man, her peace it was all unraveling, and Gloria was at the center of it.

Marcus came in, sitting beside her. "Britt, I'm just tryna help. You gettin' worked up over her, and it's makin' things worse."

"She's ruining my life, Marcus!" Brittany snapped, tears streaming down her face. "And you just standin' there like it ain't happenin'!"

Marcus sighed, rubbing the back of his neck. "I just don't see what you see, Britt. Maybe she ain't doin' it on purpose."

Brittany stared at him, her heart breaking. Even he didn't believe her.

As she lay in bed that night, Brittany felt more alone than ever. The walls seemed to close in around her, her thoughts racing. She didn't know how much more she could take, but one thing was clear: Gloria wasn't going to stop until she had taken everything.

And Brittany wasn't sure she could stop her.

# Chapter 6: Career Sabotage

Brittany stared at her computer screen, her fingers hovering over the keyboard. The deadline for her biggest project of the quarter was just hours away, and the pressure was unbearable. Usually, she thrived under pressure, but today felt different. The buzzing whispers around the office, the sidelong glances from her coworkers something wasn't right.

"Hey, Britt," came a soft voice behind her. She turned to see Gloria, holding two coffee cups. "Thought you could use a pick-me-up."

Brittany forced a smile, trying to hide the unease bubbling in her chest. "Thanks, Glo. Appreciate it."

Gloria set the cup on Brittany's desk, her eyes scanning the clutter of papers and sticky notes. "This the big project, huh?" she asked, her voice sweet but tinged with curiosity.

"Yeah," Brittany replied, turning back to her screen. "Got a lot ridin' on this one."

Gloria leaned in slightly, her tone dropping. "Well, if you need help, just holler. You know I got your back."

Brittany nodded, but something about the way Gloria lingered made her stomach twist. She felt like a rabbit with a fox circling its den.

By lunchtime, the office buzz had grown louder. Brittany caught snippets of conversations as she walked past the breakroom her name mentioned more times than she liked.

"Did you hear what Gloria said about that project?" one coworker whispered. "She's been picking up the slack for Brittany all week."

"Yeah, I heard," another replied. "Wonder if management knows."

Brittany froze mid-step, her blood running cold. *Picking up the slack?* That was a lie, and she knew it. Gloria hadn't done a damn thing for the project, but here she was spinning her web, planting seeds of doubt.

She clenched her fists, forcing herself to walk away. Confronting them now would only make her look worse. She needed to stay focused and finish her work. The truth would come out eventually or so she hoped.

Later that afternoon, Brittany was called into her boss's office. The air felt heavy as she stepped inside, the door clicking shut behind her.

"Brittany, we need to talk," Mr. Coleman said, his voice calm but firm. He gestured for her to sit, his eyes scanning a folder on his desk.

"What's goin' on?" she asked, trying to keep her voice steady.

"There have been some... concerns brought to my attention about your performance on the current project," he said, leaning forward. "I've heard from multiple people that you've been disorganized, missing deadlines, and that Gloria has had to step in to keep things on track."

Brittany's jaw dropped. "What? That's not true! I've been workin' my ass off on this project, and Gloria ain't had nothin' to do with it."

Mr. Coleman raised an eyebrow. "Gloria provided me with documentation showing that she's been assisting with key components. She's even outlined areas where she's had to correct errors."

Brittany's heart pounded. "Errors? I ain't made no damn errors! She's lyin'!"

"Brittany," Mr. Coleman said, his tone firm. "I need you to take accountability. This project is critical for the company, and if it fails, it falls on you."

The words hit her like a sledgehammer. She felt the walls closing in, her chest tightening with panic. Gloria had set her up, and now she was on the verge of losing everything.

Back at her desk, Brittany's hands trembled as she typed furiously, trying to salvage what was left of the project. She replayed the conversation with her boss over and over, each word cutting deeper. She knew Gloria was behind this, but proving it felt impossible. Gloria had played her cards perfectly, positioning herself as the hero while painting Brittany as the problem.

"Britt," Gloria's voice called out, pulling her from her thoughts. Brittany looked up to see her standing by the cubicle wall, a concerned expression plastered across her face.

"I heard you had a rough meeting with Mr. Coleman," Gloria said softly. "I'm so sorry. I didn't mean for things to get this far."

Brittany stared at her, her blood boiling. "Get this far? You mean you didn't mean to get caught."

Gloria's eyes widened, her voice dropping to a whisper. "Britt, I don't know what you're implying, but I'm only tryin' to help. If I overstepped, I'm sorry."

Brittany clenched her fists, fighting the urge to explode. "You ain't sorry. You tryna make me look bad, and you damn near succeeded."

Gloria tilted her head, her voice syrupy sweet. "I think you're just stressed. Maybe take a step back and let me handle the rest. It's okay to ask for help, you know."

Brittany's vision blurred with rage as Gloria walked away, her steps light and confident. She wanted to scream, to tear the whole office apart, but she couldn't. All she could do was sit there, stewing in her anger and humiliation.

Over the next week, the fallout from the project consumed Brittany's life. The final presentation had gone poorly, with errors mysteriously popping up that she knew weren't hers. Gloria swooped in to "save the day," delivering last-minute fixes that won her praise from management.

"Gloria really stepped up," one coworker commented as Brittany walked past. "She's a real team player."

The words were like knives to her chest. Brittany felt like she was drowning, her confidence eroding with each passing day. She started second-guessing herself, wondering if maybe she really *was* slipping.

"Yo, Britt," Marcus said one night as they sat on the couch. "You been real quiet lately. What's goin' on?"

"Work's just been... a lot," she muttered, her voice barely audible.

Marcus frowned, pulling her close. "You wanna talk about it?"

Brittany shook her head, tears welling up in her eyes. How could she explain that her life was unraveling and the person pulling the strings was someone she had let into her world? Even Marcus had started to seem distant, his once unwavering support now laced with subtle doubts.

"You gotta stop lettin' this get to you," he said softly. "Maybe Gloria ain't the problem. Maybe it's just the stress."

His words stung more than she expected. Even Marcus was questioning her now.

By the end of the week, Brittany felt like a ghost in her own life. Her friends had drifted, her coworkers whispered behind her back, and her boss seemed to have lost faith in her. Gloria, meanwhile, shined brighter than ever, her star rising on the foundation of Brittany's downfall.

As she stared at her reflection that night, her eyes burning with anger and determination, she made a silent vow: *This ain't over. Not by a long shot.*

# Chapter 7: Closer to Marcus

The faint hum of the barbershop buzzed as Marcus leaned back in his chair, his usual Saturday ritual in full effect. The clippers whirred against his head, and the scent of aftershave mingled with the sounds of old-school hip-hop playing in the background. It was one of the few places where he could relax, away from the chaos that had become his life lately.

"Yo, man," his barber, Trey, said, tilting Marcus's head to the side. "You good? You been lookin' stressed lately."

Marcus sighed, running a hand over his face. "Yeah, just... relationship shit, you feel me?"

Trey chuckled, shaking his head. "Ain't it always? What Britt got you caught up in now?"

Marcus didn't answer right away, staring at his reflection in the mirror. He loved Brittany always had. But lately, things between them had been... off. She'd been distant, angry, snapping at him for things that didn't make sense. And then there was Gloria.

Later that afternoon, Marcus was back at the auto shop where he worked. The sound of tools clinking and engines revving filled the garage. He was under the hood of a car, wiping his hands with a rag, when he heard a voice behind him.

"Marcus?"

He turned, his eyebrows shooting up in surprise. "Gloria? What you doin' here?"

She smiled, looking almost out of place in the greasy, chaotic environment. Her hair in a bun, her outfit casual but carefully put together. She held a small bag in her hands, lifting it slightly. "Britt told me you like these energy drinks, so I thought I'd bring you one. Just a lil' thank-you for always bein' so nice."

Marcus hesitated before taking the bag. "Uh, thanks. But you ain't had to do that."

"It's no problem," she said quickly, her smile never faltering. "I actually wanted to talk to you... about Brittany."

At the mention of her name, Marcus stiffened. "What about Britt?"

Gloria sighed, her expression softening. "I'm just worried about her, that's all. She hasn't been herself lately, and I thought maybe you'd noticed it too."

Marcus frowned, wiping his hands on the rag. "What you mean?"

"She's been so... on edge," Gloria said, her voice low and concerned. "She lashes out at me sometimes, and I don't even know what I did wrong. I feel like she's pushing everyone away."

Marcus's jaw tightened. He hated to admit it, but Gloria wasn't entirely wrong. Brittany had been acting different, distant. But hearing it from Gloria made his stomach twist.

"She got a lot goin' on," Marcus said, his tone defensive. "Work stress, personal shit. It's a lot to deal with."

"I get that," Gloria said, nodding. "But it's not just stress, Marcus. She's been spreading rumors about me to the group, saying I'm tryna take her place or some crazy stuff. I don't know what I did to make her feel that way."

Marcus stared at her, his mind racing. He knew Brittany had issues with Gloria, but was it really that deep? He didn't know what to believe anymore.

That evening, Marcus sat on the couch, his mind replaying the conversation with Gloria. He didn't want to doubt Brittany, but the cracks in their relationship were becoming harder to ignore.

When Brittany walked through the door, her face was tired, her eyes heavy. She dropped her bag by the door and kicked off her shoes, collapsing onto the couch beside him.

"Long day?" Marcus asked, handing her a bottle of water.

"Yeah," she muttered, taking a sip. "Work's been a mess, and I'm just... over it."

Marcus hesitated, the words hanging on the tip of his tongue. Finally, he asked, "Britt, you and Gloria... what's really goin' on?"

Brittany's head snapped up, her eyes narrowing. "What you mean?"

"I mean, she came by the shop today," Marcus said carefully. "She said you been actin' funny, sayin' stuff about her to the group."

Brittany's face hardened, her grip on the water bottle tightening. "She told you that? You really gon' believe her over me?"

"I ain't sayin' I believe her," Marcus said quickly. "But somethin' ain't addin' up, Britt. You been different lately."

"Because of her!" Brittany snapped, her voice rising. "She tryna take over my life, Marcus, and nobody sees it but me! She got yall wrapped around her damn finger."

Marcus leaned back, his face darkening. "Ain't nobody wrapped around nothin'. I'm just tryna figure out what's goin' on."

"What's goin' on is that she's a snake," Brittany said, her voice trembling. "And if you can't see that, then maybe you the one who's blind."

The silence between them was deafening, the tension thick enough to cut with a knife. Brittany stood abruptly, grabbing her bag and heading to the bedroom without another word. Marcus sat there, his hands clenched into fists. He didn't know what to think anymore.

Meanwhile, Gloria was at her apartment, a satisfied smile on her face. She sipped her wine, scrolling through her phone. The seeds she'd planted were starting to take root. Marcus was questioning Brittany now, and that was exactly what she wanted.

She'd been playing the long game, carefully weaving herself into Marcus's life. Every interaction, every conversation, was a calculated move. She didn't just want Brittany's friends or her job she wanted it all. And Marcus was the final piece.

Her phone buzzed with a text from Marcus.

*"You free to talk? I'm tryna figure some things out."*

Gloria's smile widened as she typed back. *"Of course. I'm here if you need me."*

The following week, Gloria started showing up at Marcus's lunch breaks, bringing him food and "checking in" on him. She played the role of the concerned friend perfectly, listening to his frustrations and offering subtle jabs at Brittany that sounded like genuine advice.

"Sometimes people just need space to figure themselves out," Gloria said one afternoon as they sat in the park. "Maybe Brittany's going through something she doesn't know how to handle."

Marcus nodded, her words sinking in. He didn't want to think badly of Brittany, but the cracks were widening, and Gloria seemed to understand in a way Brittany didn't.

That night, Brittany noticed the shift. Marcus was quieter, more distant. When she tried to talk to him, he brushed her off, saying he needed time to think.

Brittany sat in the living room, her heart heavy. She knew Gloria was behind this, but how could she fight back when Marcus was already slipping away?

She grabbed her phone, scrolling through Gloria's Instagram. Every post felt like a dagger picture of her at the places Brittany loved, comments from their mutual friends hyping her up. And then there was the photo that made her stomach drop: Gloria and Marcus, laughing together in the park.

Brittany's hands shook as she stared at the screen. Gloria wasn't just invading her life she was erasing her.

As the days passed, Brittany's world continued to crumble. Marcus became colder, their arguments more frequent. Gloria, meanwhile, grew bolder, her presence looming over every part of Brittany's life.

But Brittany wasn't ready to give up. She was losing everything, but she still had her fire. And she was ready to burn Gloria's world to the ground.

# Chapter 8: The Warning

The steady hum of the laundromat's fluorescent lights buzzed in Brittany's ears as she sat, scrolling mindlessly through her phone. The rhythmic thump of the dryers spinning behind her should've been comforting, but her thoughts were too chaotic. She had come here to escape, to breathe, but even now, Gloria's shadow loomed over her every move.

Her phone vibrated in her hand, snapping her back to reality. The notification read: *Message request from NiaMona22.* Brittany frowned, tapping it open. The message was short but unsettling.

*"Hey, I think you need to know something about Gloria. Hit me up."*

Brittany stared at the screen, her stomach tightening. She didn't recognize the name, but curiosity got the better of her. She typed back: *"Who is this?"*

Almost immediately, the response came: *"I'm someone who's dealt with her before. Can we talk?"*

Ten minutes later, Brittany found herself sitting in her car outside the laundromat, phone pressed to her ear. The voice on the other end was calm but carried an edge that sent chills down Brittany's spine.

"I don't know how you know her, but if Gloria's in your life, you need to watch yourself," the woman said. "She ain't who she pretend to be."

"What you mean?" Brittany asked, gripping the steering wheel tightly.

"She did the same shit to me," the woman Nia explained. "Back in Philly. She came into my world, actin' all sweet and innocent, like she just needed a friend. Next thing I know, she was copyin' me my clothes, my man, even my damn job."

Brittany's heart pounded as Nia's words mirrored everything she'd been experiencing. "What happened?"

"She turned everybody against me," Nia said bitterly. "Had people thinkin' I was crazy, jealous. Then she made her move. Took my man, spread lies at work, and left me with nothin'. She's a parasite, girl. She latch on, suck you dry, and then move on to her next target."

Brittany's mouth went dry. "How you know she doin' it to me?"

"I saw her pop up in one of my mutuals' stories," Nia replied. "Did some diggin', found out y'all was connected. Thought I should warn you before it's too late."

Brittany's hands trembled as she listened, the puzzle pieces clicking into place. This wasn't just paranoia this was a pattern.

That night, Brittany sat in her living room, replaying the conversation in her mind. The weight of Nia's words settled heavily on her chest. Gloria wasn't just some insecure girl seeking validation she was calculated, dangerous.

Brittany pulled out her phone, scrolling through her contacts until she landed on Marcus's name. She hesitated before dialing, unsure if she could convince him of what she now knew.

"Yo," Marcus answered, his voice tired.

"We need to talk," Brittany said, her voice shaking. "It's about Gloria."

Marcus groaned softly. "Britt, not this again."

"Listen to me!" she snapped. "I talked to somebody who knew her. She's done this shit before to other people. She ruins lives, Marcus. She's doin' it to me right now."

"Who'd you talk to?" he asked, his tone skeptical.

"Her name's Nia," Brittany replied. "She said Gloria did the same thing to her in Philly. Took her man, her friends, everything."

Marcus sighed. "And you believe this random chick?"

"Yes!" Brittany said, her frustration boiling over. "Because everything she said lines up with what's been happenin'! Gloria's manipulative. She's dangerous."

There was a long pause on the other end of the line. Finally, Marcus said, "Look, Britt, I don't know what's goin' on with you, but this whole thing with Gloria... it's too much. Maybe you need to step back, take a break or somethin.'"

Brittany's heart sank. "You really don't believe me?"

"It ain't about believin' or not," Marcus said softly. "It's just... you been so caught up in this, it's messin' with you. Maybe you should focus on you for a while."

Tears burned in Brittany's eyes as she hung up, her chest heaving with anger and despair. Marcus was slipping further away, and Gloria was tightening her grip on everything Brittany held dear.

The next day, Brittany met Tanisha at their favorite coffee spot. She needed someone to confide in, someone who might actually listen.

"Girl, you lookin' stressed," Tanisha said as Brittany sat down. "What's goin' on?"

Brittany leaned in, her voice low. "I talked to somebody who knew Gloria. She told me Gloria's done this same shit before back in Philly."

Tanisha raised an eyebrow. "For real?"

"She copied her, turned people against her, took her man, and left her with nothin,'" Brittany said, her voice trembling. "Sound familiar?"

Tanisha nodded slowly, her expression darkening. "Yeah, it do. But how you know this girl ain't just hatin'?"

"Because everything she said lines up, T," Brittany replied. "Gloria ain't just some random chick. She's dangerous."

Tanisha sat back, her lips pressed into a thin line. "So what you gon' do?"

Brittany sighed. "I don't know. Marcus don't believe me. Half the crew think I'm crazy. It's like I'm fightin' a ghost nobody else can see."

Tanisha reached across the table, squeezing Brittany's hand. "I got your back, Britt. You ain't fightin' alone."

That evening, Brittany paced her apartment, her mind racing. She knew she couldn't keep this to herself. If nobody else believed her, she'd have to gather proof something undeniable.

She grabbed her laptop, pulling up Gloria's social media. Scrolling through her posts, she looked for anything that might link her to Philly, to Nia, to the lies she'd spun before.

Then she saw it a photo from two years ago, tagged in Philadelphia. The caption read: *"New beginnings are everything ◈."*

Brittany's pulse quickened. She clicked on the tag, scrolling through the comments until she found one from a user named *NiaMona22*: *"More like new victims ◈."*

Her heart raced as she screenshotted the comment, feeling a surge of determination. She wasn't crazy, and she wasn't alone. Gloria had a history, and Brittany was going to expose her.

But as she closed her laptop, a knock at the door made her freeze. She glanced at the clock 9:47 PM. Her stomach twisted.

She moved slowly toward the door, peeking through the peephole. Her blood ran cold when she saw Gloria standing there, a sweet smile on her face.

"Brittany?" Gloria called softly. "You home? I just wanted to check on you."

Brittany's hand hovered over the doorknob, her mind racing. She didn't answer, stepping back silently. After a few moments, Gloria's shadow disappeared, but the unease lingered.

That night, Brittany couldn't sleep. She lay awake, her heart pounding as she replayed the day's events. The pieces were falling into place, but the game was far from over. Gloria was playing a dangerous game, and Brittany knew she needed to act fast before she became the next victim.

# Chapter 9: Rock Bottom

The rain tapped against the window like a thousand tiny fingers, its rhythm the only sound in Brittany's dark apartment. She sat curled up on the couch, staring at her phone screen. It was dead silent, not a single notification, not one missed call. The world that had once revolved around her had gone still, empty. Gloria had taken everything.

Her chest tightened as she scrolled through her contacts. Tanisha's name stared back at her, the little green "active" dot mocking her. She'd already called five times this week, but Tanisha wasn't picking up. None of them were. It was like she'd been erased, and the more she thought about it, the more it felt like maybe she had.

She tossed her phone onto the coffee table, letting out a bitter laugh. "Ain't this some shit," she muttered, her voice hoarse. "Got me sittin' here talkin' to myself like I'm crazy."

The truth was, she *felt* crazy. Gloria's games had burrowed so deep into her life that Brittany wasn't sure where the lies ended and the truth began. Every time she tried to piece things together, she found herself second-guessing everything her memories, her instincts, even her own damn sanity.

She thought about Marcus, about how cold he'd been the last time they talked. He'd barely looked at her, his tone clipped and distant.

"Britt, I need space," he'd said, his eyes glued to the floor. "This shit with Gloria... it's too much."

Space. That word echoed in her mind like a cruel joke. Gloria hadn't just taken her friends she'd taken *him*, too. Brittany could still see the way Gloria looked at him, that fake-ass concern plastered across her face. And Marcus had fallen for it, hook, line, and sinker.

The knock at the door startled her. She froze, her heart hammering in her chest. For a split second, hope flickered in her maybe it was Tanisha, or even Marcus, coming to check on her. But when she looked through the peephole, her stomach dropped.

Gloria.

Brittany's fingers clenched around the doorknob, her breathing shallow. She didn't move, didn't say a word. She hoped Gloria would think she wasn't home, but the knock came again, louder this time.

"Brittany?" Gloria's voice was soft, almost sweet. "I just wanna talk."

Brittany stepped back from the door, her hands shaking. She didn't trust herself to open it, didn't trust what she might do if she saw Gloria's face.

"I know you're in there," Gloria said, her tone turning colder. "We can't keep avoidin' each other like this."

Brittany's blood boiled at the nerve of her. Avoiding her? Gloria was the one who had torn her life apart, and now she wanted to act like they were just two friends having a little spat?

She stayed silent, waiting until she heard Gloria's footsteps retreat down the hall. But even when the sound of her heels faded, the tension in Brittany's body didn't.

The next morning, Brittany dragged herself out of bed, her limbs heavy like lead. She hadn't eaten in two days, and her reflection in the mirror was almost unrecognizable. Her skin looked dull, her eyes hollow, her usual glow replaced by shadows.

She tried to pull herself together, throwing on a hoodie and leggings before heading out to the corner store. The air outside was damp and heavy, the kind that clung to your skin and made you feel like you were suffocating. It matched her mood perfectly.

Inside the store, she grabbed a bottle of water and a pack of gum, her mind too numb to think about real food. As she stood in line, she heard whispers behind her.

"Ain't that Brittany? She lookin' rough."

"She used to be that girl, now look at her. Sad."

Brittany's hands tightened around the water bottle, her jaw clenching. She didn't turn around, didn't give them the satisfaction of seeing her react. But their words sliced through her, another reminder of how far she'd fallen.

Back at home, Brittany sat on the floor of her living room, the bottle of water unopened beside her. She thought about Nia's warning, about how Gloria had done this to other people before. She thought about Marcus, about Tanisha, about everyone who used to be in her corner. They were all gone now, swallowed up by Gloria's lies.

The weight of it all crushed her, and for the first time in a long time, Brittany let herself cry. The sobs wracked her body, the sound raw and guttural. She cried for everything she'd lost, for the person she used to be, for the life that was slipping further out of reach with every passing day.

When the tears finally stopped, she sat there in the silence, her face buried in her hands. She felt empty, like there was nothing left inside her but pain.

Her phone buzzed, pulling her out of her thoughts. She grabbed it, her heart sinking when she saw Marcus's name. For a second, she debated not answering, but she couldn't help herself.

"Hello?" Her voice was barely above a whisper.

"Britt," Marcus said, his tone cautious. "We need to talk."

She sat up straighter, her heart pounding. "About what?"

"About us. About everything," he said. "Can I come by?"

Brittany hesitated, her mind racing. Part of her wanted to tell him no, to push him away before he could hurt her again. But the other part the part that still loved him couldn't let go.

"Yeah," she said finally. "Come over."

When Marcus arrived, the tension between them was palpable. He stood in the doorway, his hands shoved in his pockets, his eyes darting around the apartment like he didn't recognize it.

"You okay?" he asked, his voice soft.

Brittany shrugged, crossing her arms over her chest. "What you wanna talk about?"

Marcus sighed, running a hand over his head. "I don't even know where to start."

"Try the truth," Brittany snapped. "You been spendin' all this time with Gloria, believin' her lies. You ain't even givin' me a chance."

"I ain't takin' sides," Marcus said, his tone defensive. "I just... I don't know what to believe anymore."

Brittany felt her chest tighten, the tears threatening to spill again. "How can you not see what she's doin'? She's manipulative, Marcus. She's been settin' me up from the start."

Marcus looked at her, his eyes filled with something she couldn't quite place. "You really think she's that dangerous?"

Brittany nodded, her voice trembling. "I know she is."

He stared at her for a long moment before finally saying, "Then prove it."

After he left, Brittany sat in the dark, her mind racing. She had nothing left to lose, and everything to fight for. Gloria had pushed her to the edge, but Brittany wasn't about to let her win.

She grabbed her phone and pulled up Nia's number. As it rang, she took a deep breath, steeling herself for what was to come.

When Nia answered, Brittany's voice was steady. "This bitch is trying to ruin me. Tell me everything."

# Chapter 10: Unraveling the Truth

Brittany sat at her kitchen table, her laptop open and glowing in the dim light. The room was silent except for the rhythmic tapping of her nails against the table. She hadn't slept, hadn't eaten, and didn't care. She was running on pure adrenaline now, fueled by one singular goal: expose Gloria for the fraud she was.

Her conversation with Nia had left her shaken but focused. Gloria wasn't just messy she was dangerous. This wasn't some petty drama. This was calculated destruction, and Brittany was done playing the victim.

She started with the basics. Gloria had mentioned being from Philly, so Brittany searched for anything that could tie her to the city. Hours passed as she combed through social media profiles, news articles, and forum posts. Just when she was about to give up, she found it a blog post from two years ago titled *"The Fake Friend Who Destroyed My Life."*

The post was written by someone named Layla, and as Brittany read, her blood turned cold. Layla described how Gloria, under a different name, had come into her life, wormed her way into her circle, and then systematically dismantled everything. The details were eerily similar to Brittany's experience: the copying, the lies, the gaslighting.

But it didn't stop there. Layla had included screenshots, texts, photos, and even a restraining order she'd filed against Gloria. Brittany's hands shook as she saved everything to a folder on her laptop. She finally had proof, but the weight of it made her stomach churn.

She couldn't do this alone. She needed allies, people who would believe her and help her stop Gloria. Her first thought was Marcus, but she hesitated. He'd been so distant lately, so caught up in Gloria's web, that she wasn't sure he'd even listen. But she had to try.

Grabbing her phone, she texted him: *"We need to talk. It's important."*

Minutes felt like hours as she waited for his response. Finally, her phone buzzed.

*"I'll come by after work."*

When Marcus arrived, Brittany wasted no time. She pulled up the folder on her laptop and turned the screen toward him. "Look at this," she said, her voice trembling. "Look at what she's done."

Marcus sat down, his brows furrowed as he scrolled through the evidence. At first, he seemed skeptical, but the further he read, the more his expression darkened.

"This... this can't be real," he said finally, his voice low.

"It's real," Brittany said firmly. "She's done this before, Marcus. To Layla, to Nia, to God knows how many other people. She finds somebody to latch onto, destroys their life, and then moves on."

Marcus leaned back, running a hand over his face. "Damn. I... I don't even know what to say."

"Say you believe me," Brittany said, her voice breaking. "Say you'll help me stop her."

He looked at her, his eyes filled with a mix of guilt and determination. "I believe you, Britt. I'm sorry I didn't see it sooner."

With Marcus on her side, Brittany felt a spark of hope. But they still had a long way to go. Gloria had ingrained herself so deeply into Brittany's world that pulling her out wouldn't be easy. They needed a plan, and they needed backup.

The next day, Brittany reached out to Tanisha. She didn't know if her friend would listen, but she had to try.

"Meet me at the café," Brittany texted. "It's urgent."

Tanisha showed up twenty minutes later, her expression wary. "What's this about, Britt? I ain't tryna get caught up in no more drama."

"It's not drama," Brittany said, pulling out her laptop. "It's the truth."

She showed Tanisha everything the blog post, the screenshots, the restraining order. Tanisha's eyes widened as she read, her jaw tightening.

"This... this is wild," Tanisha said, shaking her head. "I knew somethin' was off about her, but this? This is some next-level shit."

"Exactly," Brittany said. "I need your help, T. We gotta show the others. They need to know who she really is."

Tanisha hesitated, biting her lip. "You sure this ain't gon' backfire? She seem real good at spinnin' shit."

"That's why we gotta hit her with the facts," Brittany said. "No more he-said-she-said. Just straight-up proof."

Together, they called a meeting with their remaining friends. It wasn't easy most of them were still under Gloria's spell, and convincing them to even show up took some serious effort. But by the time they all gathered in Tanisha's living room, Brittany was ready.

She stood at the front of the room, her laptop hooked up to the TV. The folder of evidence was open, ready to be presented.

"I know y'all think I've been trippin'," Brittany began, her voice steady but firm. "I know Gloria's been tellin' y'all that I'm jealous or crazy or whatever. But tonight, I'm gonna show you the truth."

One by one, she went through the evidence. The blog post. The screenshots. The restraining order. The room was silent as her friends read and listened, their expressions shifting from confusion to shock to anger.

When she finished, Brittany took a deep breath. "This is who she is," she said. "She's been playin' all of us. But now we know, and we can stop her."

For a moment, nobody spoke. Then Kelly, who had been one of Gloria's biggest supporters, stood up. "I can't believe I fell for her bullshit," she said, her voice shaking. "Britt, I'm sorry. I should've had your back."

One by one, the others expressed their regret, their anger at being manipulated. Brittany felt a weight lift off her shoulders, but she knew the battle wasn't over yet.

Later that night, as Brittany sat in her apartment, she felt a sense of calm for the first time in weeks. She wasn't alone anymore. She had Marcus, Tanisha, and her friends by her side. They were ready to confront Gloria, to expose her for who she really was.

But as Brittany stared out the window, watching the city lights twinkle in the distance, a sense of unease crept in. Gloria wouldn't go down without a fight. She was too calculated, too dangerous.

Brittany's phone buzzed with a new message. She picked it up, her heart sinking when she saw the sender.

*"You think you slick, don't you?"*

It was Gloria.

Brittany's hands trembled as she read the message.

# Chapter 11: A Dangerous Confrontation

The bar was alive with the sound of music, clinking glasses, and laughter. It was one of those Friday nights when everyone wanted to be seen, the type of night that Brittany used to own. Now, she sat at a corner table, her jaw tight, her eyes locked on Gloria, who was holding conversation in the center of the room like she was the queen of the damn city.

Brittany's hands clenched around her glass as she watched Gloria laugh with *her* friends, dressed in an outfit so similar to one Brittany had worn a month ago it felt like déjà vu. Gloria's smile was radiant, her voice carrying above the crowd, dripping with charm. Everyone was eating it up, just like always.

Tanisha sat across from Brittany, her face grim. "You sure you wanna do this here?" she asked, her voice low. "This shit could backfire real bad."

"I ain't got no choice," Brittany hissed. "She been playin' me too long, T. It's time everybody sees her for who she really is."

Tanisha didn't look convinced, but she nodded. "Aight. Just don't lose your cool."

Brittany stood, her heart pounding as she crossed the room. The crowd seemed to part for her, heads turning as she approached. By the time she reached Gloria, the noise had died down, all eyes on them.

"Brittany!" Gloria said, her smile wide and fake as hell. "Didn't expect to see you here."

Brittany ignored the greeting, her voice cutting through the room like a knife. "We need to talk."

Gloria's eyes narrowed slightly, but her smile didn't waver. "Sure. What's up?"

"Right here," Brittany said, her voice rising. "In front of everybody."

The crowd murmured, the tension crackling like static electricity. Gloria tilted her head, feigning confusion. "Is somethin' wrong?"

"You damn right somethin's wrong," Brittany snapped. "You been lyin', manipulatin', and settin' me up from day one. And I got proof."

The room went silent as Brittany pulled out her phone, holding it up for everyone to see. "This is her," she said, scrolling through the screenshots she'd saved. "This is what she did to other people. Philly, Jersey everywhere she been, she leaves a trail of lies and destruction."

Gloria's face paled for a split second before she recovered, her voice soft and full of concern. "Brittany... what are you talking about?"

"Don't play dumb bitch!" Brittany shouted, her anger boiling over. "You know exactly what I'm talkin' about. You been copyin' me, takin' my life, turnin' my friends against me."

The crowd shifted uneasily, their eyes darting between Brittany and Gloria. Tanisha stood at the edge of the group, her arms crossed, her expression unreadable.

Gloria sighed, shaking her head. "Britt, I don't know what's goin' on with you, but this ain't it. I thought we were friends."

"Friends?" Brittany scoffed. "You don't know the first thing about bein' a friend."

Gloria's eyes glistened, and her voice trembled just enough to sound genuine. "I've been nothin' but supportive of you, Britt. If you feel like I've done somethin' wrong, I'm sorry, but this... this is too much."

The shift was subtle, but Brittany felt it like a punch to the gut. The crowd started to lean toward Gloria, their sympathy turning in her direction. Kelly stepped forward, her face a mix of confusion and concern.

"Britt, maybe we should talk about this later," Kelly said gently. "You seem... upset."

"I *am* upset!" Brittany snapped. "Y'all lettin' her fool you, just like she fooled me."

"Brittany," Gloria said, her voice low and soothing. "I think you need help."

The words hit Brittany like a slap. The room blurred around her as Gloria's calm, composed demeanor contrasted sharply with her own raw, exposed anger. The narrative was slipping away, just like it always did.

"She lyin'!" Brittany shouted, her voice cracking. "She's been lyin' this whole time!"

Gloria placed a hand on Kelly's arm, her eyes full of fake concern. "I just want her to get the help she needs. This ain't the Brittany I know."

The crowd began to murmur, their whispers slicing through Brittany's ears like daggers. She turned to Tanisha, her last hope, but even Tanisha looked hesitant, her arms wrapped tightly around herself.

"Don't look at me like that, T," Brittany pleaded. "You know I'm tellin' the truth."

Tanisha hesitated before finally saying, "I don't know, Britt. Maybe... maybe this ain't the way."

Brittany's heart shattered. She felt the walls closing in, the weight of isolation crushing her. Gloria had won. Again.

The confrontation ended with Brittany storming out of the bar, her vision blurred by tears of rage and humiliation. She could still hear the murmurs behind her, the sound of Gloria's voice soothing the crowd like a snake charmer.

Outside, the cool night air hit her face, but it did little to calm her. She leaned against the wall, her chest heaving as she tried to catch her breath.

"Yo, Britt!" a voice called. She turned to see Marcus jogging toward her, his expression conflicted. "What the hell was that?"

"You saw it," Brittany said bitterly. "You saw how she twisted everything."

Marcus sighed, running a hand over his head. "Look, I get that you upset, but you can't be doin' this shit in public. You makin' yourself look crazy."

Brittany laughed, the sound hollow and bitter. "Crazy? That's what she wants you to think. That's what she's been doin' this whole time."

Marcus hesitated, his eyes searching hers. "I just... I don't know, Britt. Maybe you should let this go."

"Let it go?" Brittany stepped closer, her voice trembling with fury. "She took my friends, my job, my life. And now you tellin' me to let it go?"

Marcus didn't respond, his silence cutting deeper than words ever could. Brittany turned away, her tears falling freely now. She felt like she was drowning, the weight of everything dragging her under.

Back at her apartment, Brittany collapsed onto the couch, her body shaking with sobs. She had fought so hard, put everything on the line, and still, Gloria had come out on top. Her friends were gone, her reputation in shambles, and Marcus her rock was slipping further away with each passing day.

She thought about the girl she used to be, the girl who lit up every room she walked into. That girl was gone now, replaced by someone she barely recognized.

As she sat there in the dark, a cold resolve settled over her. Gloria might have won this round, but Brittany wasn't done yet. If nobody else was going to fight for her, she'd fight for herself.

She grabbed her laptop, opening the folder of evidence once more. This time, she wasn't just gathering proof. She was preparing for war.

# Chapter 12: The Threat

The streets were quiet that night, the usual hum of life muted under the blanket of darkness. Brittany's steps echoed as she walked from the corner store, her bag of groceries feeling heavier than it should. Every shadow felt like it was watching her, every sound amplified in her mind. She couldn't shake the feeling that something wasn't right.

Her phone buzzed in her pocket, the sudden vibration making her jump. She pulled it out, squinting at the screen. It was an unknown number.

*"I see you."*

Brittany froze, her heart hammering. She spun around, her eyes darting up and down the street. Nobody was there, but the air felt suffocating, like it was closing in on her.

She typed back quickly, her fingers trembling. *"Who is this?"*

The response came instantly. *"You know who."*

Brittany made it home in record time, locking the door behind her and triple-checking the bolts. She leaned against it, trying to catch her breath, her mind racing. She knew it was Gloria. She didn't need confirmation. The woman had gone from subtle manipulation to full-blown terror.

Her phone buzzed again, and this time, it was a call. The same unknown number. She hesitated before answering, her voice shaking as she said, "What do you want?"

Laughter greeted her on the other end, cold and cruel. "Brittany, Brittany," Gloria said, her tone mocking. "You really thought you could beat me?"

"What the fuck is your problem, Gloria?" Brittany snapped, her fear giving way to anger. "Why you doin' this?"

"Because I can," Gloria replied, her voice dripping with malice. "Because everything you have should've been mine. Your friends, your job, even Marcus... they all deserve better. And let's face it, Britt you were never good enough to have them."

Brittany's grip on the phone tightened. "You're sick."

"No, I'm just better," Gloria said smoothly. "And now? I'm gonna make sure everyone sees it. You think you're scared now? Just wait."

The line went dead, leaving Brittany standing in the silence of her apartment, her blood running cold.

The next day, Brittany tried to shake off the conversation, but the fear lingered, a constant presence in the back of her mind. She met up with Tanisha, needing to talk to someone, anyone, who might understand.

"Yo, Britt, you look like you ain't slept in days," Tanisha said as they sat in a booth at their usual diner.

"I haven't," Brittany admitted, her voice low. "She called me last night, T. Straight up threatened me."

Tanisha's eyes widened. "She said what?"

"She said she wants my life. That she's gonna make me disappear." Brittany's hands shook as she spoke. "T, I don't know what to do. She's everywhere, and now she ain't even tryna hide it."

Tanisha leaned back, her face grim. "You gotta go to the cops, Britt. This shit ain't no game."

"And tell them what?" Brittany snapped. "That this chick copyin' me and tryna ruin my life? They'll laugh me out the precinct."

Tanisha sighed, shaking her head. "Then you gotta protect yourself. Don't let her catch you slippin.'"

That night, Brittany sat in her living room, clutching a knife she'd pulled from the kitchen drawer. The blinds were drawn, every light in the apartment turned on. She was on edge, her body coiled tight like a spring.

The knock on the door came around midnight. It was soft at first, then louder, more insistent. Brittany's stomach dropped.

"Brittany," Gloria's voice called. "I know you're in there. Open up."

Brittany didn't move, her heart pounding so hard she thought it might burst.

"Don't make me break this door down," Gloria said, her tone light but menacing. "We need to talk."

Brittany's grip on the knife tightened as she stood, her feet moving toward the door despite her fear. She peeked through the peephole, her breath catching at the sight of Gloria standing there, her smile calm and cold.

"I'm not scared of you," Brittany said through the door, though her voice betrayed her.

Gloria laughed, the sound chilling. "Oh, you should be. You really think you can stop me, Britt? You're just a stepping stone, a little bump in my road."

"What do you want from me?" Brittany demanded, her voice trembling.

"I want you gone," Gloria said simply. "But if you won't disappear on your own, I'll help you."

The threat sent a jolt of terror through Brittany, but before she could respond, there was a loud crash. Gloria had kicked the door, the sound reverberating through the apartment.

Brittany stumbled back, her heart racing as the door shook under Gloria's assault. She held the knife in front of her, her breath coming in short gasps.

The door gave way on the third kick, swinging open to reveal Gloria, her face twisted with a mix of triumph and malice.

"You really thought stop me?" Gloria sneered, stepping inside.

"Get the fuck out!" Brittany screamed, holding the knife up.

Gloria smirked, her eyes gleaming. "What you gonna do, Britt? Stab me? You ain't got it in you."

Brittany's hands shook, but she didn't lower the knife. "Try me."

Gloria took another step forward, her voice dropping to a dangerous whisper. "You're pathetic. Nobody believes you. Nobody cares. And soon? Nobody's gonna remember you."

The rage and fear bubbling inside Brittany reached a boiling point. She lunged forward, the knife slicing through the air between them. Gloria stepped back just in time, the blade narrowly missing her.

"You crazy bitch!" Gloria shouted, grabbing a lamp from the nearby table and swinging it at Brittany.

The lamp connected with Brittany's shoulder, sending her crashing to the ground. Pain shot through her, but adrenaline pushed her to her feet. She swung the knife again, this time grazing Gloria's arm. Blood bloomed on her sleeve, but Gloria didn't flinch.

"You think this scares me?" Gloria snarled, her eyes wild. "That's light work."

The struggle felt like it lasted hours, though it was only minutes. By the time Gloria fled, slamming the broken door behind her, Brittany was left shaking and gasping for air. Her apartment was in shambles, her body bruised and aching, but she was alive.

She sank to the floor, the knife still clutched in her hand. Tears streamed down her face as the reality of what had just happened sank in. Gloria wasn't just a threat anymore. She was a predator, and Brittany was her prey.

As she sat there, her phone buzzed. It was a text from an unknown number.

*"You got lucky tonight. But next time, I won't miss."*

Brittany stared at the message, her blood turning to ice. This wasn't over. Not even close.

# Chapter 13: Fight for Survival

The night was thick with silence, the kind that pressed against Brittany's ears and made her feel trapped in her own apartment. She hadn't slept in days, her nerves frayed and raw. Every creak in the floorboards, every gust of wind against the windows set her heart racing. Gloria was out there, and Brittany knew she wouldn't stop until she'd taken everything.

She sat in her living room clutching a baseball bat, her only source of comfort. Her phone sat on the coffee table, Marcus's number already dialed but not called. She couldn't bring herself to reach out again, not after the last conversation where even he seemed unsure of her sanity.

Brittany glanced at the clock 2:34 a.m. The air felt heavy, suffocating. Something wasn't right. She stood and paced the room, her bat in hand, trying to shake the feeling crawling up her spine.

Then she heard it a faint noise, barely audible. A click, like a door unlocking.

Her breath caught in her throat. She froze, her eyes darting toward the hallway. The sound came again, louder this time. It was coming from her bedroom.

Brittany's grip on the bat tightened as she crept toward the hallway. Her heart pounded in her chest, each step feeling like it echoed through the apartment. She reached the doorway to her bedroom and paused, listening.

The faint sound of drawers opening and closing reached her ears, followed by a low, muttered curse. Someone was in her room.

She stepped inside, her pulse racing. At first, the room looked empty, but then she saw her closet door ajar. A shadow moved inside, and Brittany's blood turned cold.

"Gloria," she said, her voice trembling but loud. "Get the fuck outta my house."

The shadow froze, and for a moment, there was silence. Then Gloria stepped out, holding one of Brittany's scarves in her hands, her expression calm, almost amused.

"Brittany," she said, tilting her head. "I thought you were sleeping."

"What the hell are you doin'?" Brittany demanded, raising the bat. "You've lost your damn mind."

Gloria smirked, draping the scarf over her shoulders like it was hers. "Just takin' what's mine."

"This ain't your shit!" Brittany shouted, her voice breaking. "This is my life, my home. Get out before I call the cops."

Gloria's smirk faded, replaced by a cold glare. "You really think they'll believe you? They'll think you're crazy, Britt. Just like everybody else."

The tension snapped like a rubber band. Brittany lunged forward, swinging the bat. Gloria dodged it with surprising speed, the scarf falling to the floor as she grabbed Brittany's arm.

The two women struggled, their movements clumsy and chaotic. Brittany's anger fueled her, but Gloria's strength surprised her. They crashed into the dresser, knocking over a lamp that shattered on the floor.

"You think you're better than me?" Gloria hissed, her voice venomous. "You ain't shit without me."

"You're insane!" Brittany screamed, trying to shove Gloria off her. "You're a goddamn parasite!"

Gloria's hand shot out, grabbing a picture frame from the nightstand. She swung it, the glass slicing Brittany's arm. Brittany cried out, the pain sharp and immediate, but she didn't stop. She grabbed Gloria by the hair, yanking her backward.

The two women fell to the floor, grappling and throwing punches. Gloria's nails raked across Brittany's face, but Brittany countered with a hard elbow to her ribs. The room filled with the sounds of their struggle grunts, crashes, and the sharp crack of wood splintering as the bat hit the wall.

Finally, Brittany managed to pin Gloria beneath her, the bat pressed against her neck. "Why?!" Brittany screamed, tears streaming down her face. "Why you doin' this to me?!"

Gloria's lips twisted into a cruel smile, her voice low and chilling. "Because you don't deserve it. None of it. Your life should've been mine."

The words hit Brittany like a punch to the gut. She stared at Gloria, her hands trembling, the bat still pressed against her neck. For a moment, she considered ending it right there, taking back her power once and for all.

But then Gloria's knee shot up, catching Brittany in the stomach. The impact knocked the wind out of her, and she fell back, gasping for air. Gloria scrambled to her feet, her movements quick and frantic.

"You'll never be rid of me, Britt," Gloria spat, grabbing the scarf from the floor. "I'll always be one step ahead."

Before Brittany could recover, Gloria bolted for the door. Brittany stumbled after her, but by the time she reached the hallway, Gloria was gone, the front door swinging open in the night air.

Brittany slammed the door shut, locking it and shoving a chair under the handle for good measure. Her body ached, her arm bleeding, but none of that mattered. The reality of what had just happened hit her like a freight train.

She was alone. Truly alone.

She collapsed onto the couch, her hands shaking as she pressed them to her face. Her apartment was a wreck, her body battered, and her mind spinning. Gloria had pushed her to the edge, and there was no going back now.

The next morning, Brittany sat in the waiting room of a locksmith, her nerves still raw. She had called in sick to work, knowing she couldn't face anyone in her current state. Her arm was bandaged, the scratches on her face stinging with every movement.

When her name was called, she stood and explained the situation to the locksmith a half-truth about a "break-in" from an "ex-friend." The man didn't ask questions, just nodded and set to work.

By the time the new locks were installed, Brittany felt a small sense of relief, but it was fleeting. She knew this wasn't the end. Gloria was still out there, and as long as she was, Brittany would never truly be safe.

That night, Brittany sat at her kitchen table, staring at the knife she'd placed in front of her. She didn't know what her next move was, but one thing was certain: she couldn't keep living like this. Gloria had taken everything from her, but she wouldn't take her life not without a fight.

Her phone buzzed, and she picked it up hesitantly. It was a text from an unknown number.

*"Nice try, Britt. See you soon."*

Brittany's hands shook as she stared at the message. Fear twisted in her gut, but alongside it was something else anger. Pure, unfiltered rage.

She wasn't going to run. She wasn't going to hide.

It was time to end this.

# Chapter 14: A Deadly Trap

The message came through late in the evening, the sky outside Brittany's window dark and heavy with rain clouds. Her phone buzzed against the table, the vibration startling her in the quiet apartment. She picked it up hesitantly, her stomach tightening when she saw the sender: Gloria.

*"Meet me. Let's settle this once and for all."*

Brittany stared at the words, her pulse quickening. She knew it was a trap. Everything about Gloria screamed danger, manipulation, and chaos. But this time, Brittany wasn't the same woman Gloria had been tormenting for months. This time, she was ready.

She responded with a simple, *"Where?"* keeping her tone neutral, calculated. She wasn't going into this blind, but she needed to know Gloria's next move.

The reply came seconds later: *"The old factory on Jefferson. Midnight. Come alone."*

Brittany's heart pounded as she read the message, the words dripping with menace. She couldn't shake the image of the abandoned factory, a hulking, decrepit structure that had been empty for years. It was the perfect setting for Gloria's twisted endgame.

She grabbed her bag, her mind racing as she packed: her phone, a flashlight, pepper spray, and a small knife she'd taken from the kitchen. It wasn't much, but it was better than nothing.

The drive to the factory was eerily quiet, the rain tapping against the windshield as if warning her to turn back. The streets were slick, the faint glow of streetlights reflecting off the wet pavement. Brittany gripped the steering wheel tightly, her mind replaying every moment that had led her to this point.

Gloria had taken everything from her friends, her job, her peace of mind. This confrontation wasn't just about ending Gloria's torment; it was about reclaiming her life.

She parked a block away, not wanting her car to give her away. As she approached the factory on foot, her heart pounded in her chest, each step feeling heavier than the last. The building loomed before her, its broken windows like dark, empty eyes watching her approach.

Inside, the factory was dark and damp, the air thick with the scent of mildew and rust. Brittany clicked on her flashlight, the beam cutting through the shadows as she moved cautiously through the space. The sound of dripping water echoed in the silence, each drop a reminder of how alone she was.

"Gloria!" Brittany called, her voice steady despite the fear twisting in her gut. "I'm here. Where you at?"

Her voice bounced off the walls, but there was no reply. She moved deeper into the factory, her footsteps soft on the concrete floor. Her grip tightened around the flashlight, her other hand resting on the pepper spray in her pocket.

Then she heard it a faint laugh, cold and cruel.

"You actually came," Gloria's voice rang out, the sound coming from somewhere above her. "I wasn't sure you had it in you."

Brittany spun, her flashlight sweeping the room. "Where are you?" she demanded, her voice echoing.

"Right where I need to be," Gloria replied, her tone mocking. "You've always been predictable, Britt. That's your problem."

Brittany's jaw clenched, her fear giving way to anger. "You wanted me here? Then show yourself. Stop hiding."

The sound of footsteps echoed above her, followed by the creak of metal. Brittany turned her flashlight toward the second level, catching a glimpse of Gloria's figure moving along the catwalk.

Brittany climbed the stairs cautiously, her breath shallow as she approached the second level. Gloria stood at the far end of the catwalk, her silhouette framed by the dim light filtering through a broken window. She was holding something a crowbar, its metal glinting in the faint light.

"You really think you can beat me?" Gloria said, her voice carrying over the distance. "After everything, you think you can just win?"

Brittany stepped closer, her voice cold. "I worried. I'm takin' my life back."

Gloria laughed, the sound sharp and bitter. "Your life? Sweetheart, your life has been mine for months. I own you."

"You don't own shit," Brittany snapped, pulling the pepper spray from her pocket. "This ends tonight, Gloria."

Gloria's expression twisted into a sneer. "You wanna end it? Then come and try."

The fight was sudden and violent, a blur of motion and chaos. Brittany sprayed the pepper spray, the sharp chemical mist hitting Gloria in the face. Gloria screamed, dropping the crowbar as she clawed at her eyes. Brittany didn't wait she lunged, her flashlight swinging like a club.

The blow caught Gloria across the shoulder, knocking her off balance. She stumbled but didn't fall, her rage overpowering the pain. She swung wildly, her nails raking across Brittany's arm, drawing blood.

"You think you can hurt me?" Gloria snarled, her voice dripping with venom. "You're nothing!"

Brittany ducked another swing, her heart pounding as adrenaline coursed through her veins. She grabbed the crowbar, pulling it away from Gloria and throwing it across the room.

"Get the fuck outta my life!" Brittany screamed, shoving Gloria backward.

Gloria stumbled, her foot catching on the edge of the catwalk. For a moment, time seemed to freeze as she teetered on the edge, her arms flailing. Then she fell, her scream echoing through the factory as she plummeted to the ground below.

Brittany rushed to the edge, her breath catching as she looked down. Gloria lay sprawled on the concrete floor, motionless. For a moment, Brittany thought it was over that Gloria was finally gone.

But then Gloria moved, a low groan escaping her lips as she pushed herself up on trembling arms. Blood dripped from her head, her face twisted in pain and fury.

"You... you can't win," Gloria spat, her voice weak but defiant. "I'll always come back."

Brittany stared down at her, her chest heaving. She felt a mix of relief and dread, knowing this wasn't the end. Gloria wasn't going to stop not until one of them was gone for good.

She turned and ran, her footsteps echoing as she fled the factory. She didn't look back, her only thought on getting away, on surviving.

Back in her apartment, Brittany locked the door and sank to the floor, her body trembling. She was covered in bruises, her arm still bleeding from Gloria's attack. But she was alive.

Her phone buzzed, and she grabbed it with shaking hands. It was a message from an unknown number.

*"You're lucky. But next time, I'll finish it."*

Brittany stared at the screen, her blood running cold. She knew this wasn't over. Gloria was still out there, still hunting her.

But Brittany wasn't done fighting. Not yet.

# Chapter 15: The Tables Turn

The morning light sliced through the blinds in Brittany's apartment, but it brought no warmth or comfort. She sat at her kitchen table, staring at the small pile of evidence she had collected: screenshots, notes, and photos. Her bruised arm throbbed, but the pain was a reminder that she was still here. Still fighting.

The night at the factory had shaken her, but it had also ignited something deep within a fire she hadn't felt in months. Gloria had pushed her to the brink, but Brittany wasn't about to let her win. Not now. Not ever.

Her phone buzzed, the screen lighting up with a message from Tanisha.

*"Yo, you good? Haven't heard from you since last night."*

Brittany typed back quickly. *"I'm good. Just layin' low. Shit's gettin' crazy."*

Tanisha's response came almost immediately. *"Be careful, Britt. Gloria's been runnin' her mouth, sayin' you attacked her. People out here takin' her side."*

Brittany's jaw tightened, her nails digging into the edge of the table. Gloria was spinning her web again, turning the narrative in her favor. But Brittany wasn't about to let her lies go unchecked.

She spent the rest of the day planning, her mind racing as she pieced together a way to fight back. Gloria had underestimated her, thinking she was weak, easy to manipulate. But Brittany knew how to play dirty too. She'd grown up in these streets; she knew how the game worked.

By evening, she had a plan. It was risky, but she didn't have any other options. She texted Tanisha again.

*"Need your help tonight. Can you meet me?"*

Tanisha replied quickly. *"Where at?"*

Brittany sent the location a neutral spot in a park on the west side. She couldn't risk meeting anywhere too public, not with Gloria's lies spreading like wildfire.

The park was quiet when Brittany arrived, the air crisp and tinged with the faint smell of rain. She sat on a bench near the edge of the playground, her hoodie pulled tight around her face. Her hands clenched the pepper spray in her pocket, her nerves on edge.

Tanisha arrived a few minutes later, her expression wary. "Britt, what's goin' on? You look like you ready for war."

"I am," Brittany said bluntly. "This ends tonight."

Tanisha's eyes widened. "What you mean? You tryna"

"I ain't killin' nobody," Brittany interrupted, her voice firm. "But I'm takin' back my life. I need you to have my back."

Tanisha hesitated, then nodded. "Aight. What's the plan?"

Brittany explained quickly, outlining her strategy. They were going to lure Gloria out, confront her in a way that she couldn't manipulate or escape. Brittany needed witnesses people who could see Gloria for who she truly was.

"She won't come if she thinks it's a setup," Tanisha said. "How you gon' get her to show?"

Brittany pulled out her phone, her lips curling into a grim smile. "I'll give her what she wants."

Later that night, Brittany sent the message: *"You win. I'm done fightin'. Let's meet."*

The reply came instantly. *"Where?"*

Brittany hesitated for only a second before typing: *"The old community center. Midnight. Come alone."*

The community center was a relic of the past, its faded walls and broken windows a testament to better days long gone. Brittany stood inside the empty hall, the air thick with dust and decay. She had positioned Tanisha and a few trusted friends outside, ready to call the cops if things went south.

She didn't have to wait long. The sound of footsteps echoed through the building, slow and deliberate. Brittany's heart pounded as Gloria emerged from the shadows, her smile cold and predatory.

"Well, well," Gloria said, her voice dripping with mockery. "Didn't think you'd give up this easy."

"I ain't givin' up," Brittany said, her voice steady. "I'm takin' my life back."

Gloria laughed, the sound sharp and grating. "Your life? Baby, your life *is* mine now. And there ain't nothin' you can do about it."

Brittany stepped closer, her fists clenched. "You really think you can keep this up? That nobody'll see through you?"

"They won't," Gloria said confidently. "Because I'm better at this than you'll ever be."

The confrontation escalated quickly. Gloria lunged, her hands clawing at Brittany's face. Brittany fought back, every punch and shove fueled by months of fear and anger. The two women crashed into a table, the wood splintering beneath them.

"You think you're strong?" Gloria hissed, her nails digging into Brittany's arm. "You're weak. You've always been weak."

Brittany shoved her off, her breath coming in ragged gasps. "You don't know me."

"Oh, I know you," Gloria spat, grabbing a shard of broken wood from the table. "And I know how this ends."

Before she could strike, the door burst open, the sound of heavy footsteps filling the room. Both women froze as Marcus appeared, his face a mix of fury and determination.

"Drop it, Gloria," Marcus said, his voice low and dangerous.

Gloria's eyes widened, her grip on the wood faltering. "Marcus? What are you doin' here?"

"I've been watchin'," he said, stepping closer. "Been watchin' you tear Brittany's life apart. And I'm done lettin' it happen."

Gloria's confidence wavered, her gaze darting between Marcus and Brittany. "She's lyin' to you. She's been lyin' this whole time."

"Nah," Marcus said, pulling out his phone. "I got the proof. You been slippin', Gloria. Leavin' your tracks all over the place. You think you're so smart, but you ain't."

The room was silent as Marcus played a recording a conversation between Gloria and one of her previous victims. The words were damning, exposing her lies and manipulations in brutal detail.

Gloria's face twisted in rage. "You think this changes anything?" she snarled. "I'll still win. I always win."

"Not this time," Brittany said, her voice steady. "This time, you lose."

As the cops arrived, Gloria fought tooth and nail, her screams echoing through the empty building. Brittany watched as they cuffed her, a mix of relief and exhaustion washing over her.

Marcus approached her, his expression softening. "You okay?"

Brittany nodded, her voice barely above a whisper. "I am now."

That night, Brittany sat in her apartment, the first glimmers of peace settling over her. Gloria was gone, and though the scars of her torment remained, Brittany knew she had won.

For the first time in months, she felt peace.

# Chapter 16: Rebuilding

The hum of the city felt different now, quieter somehow, like the storm had finally passed. Brittany sat on the worn steps of her apartment building, her phone in one hand and a cigarette in the other. She hadn't smoked in years, but tonight felt like an exception. She needed something to steady her nerves, even if it was just the sharp pull of nicotine in her lungs.

The news about Gloria's arrest had spread like wildfire. Social media was buzzing, her name trending for all the wrong reasons. Articles labeled her a "master manipulator," a "serial con artist," but Brittany knew that didn't even scratch the surface. Gloria was more than a manipulator she was a predator.

"Yo, Britt," Tanisha called out, pulling up in her car. The engine rumbled as she parked and stepped out, her heels clicking against the pavement. "You good?"

Brittany exhaled, the smoke curling into the night air. "I'm gettin' there."

Tanisha climbed the steps and sat beside her. "I heard about what went down. Marcus told me everything. That chick was crazy for real."

"Crazy don't even cover it," Brittany muttered, flicking the ash from her cigarette. "She damn near destroyed my life, T. I don't even know where to start pickin' up the pieces."

The first piece came the next morning when Brittany received a call from her old boss, Mr. Coleman. His tone was hesitant but apologetic.

"Brittany," he began, clearing his throat. "I just wanted to say I'm sorry for how things played out. We should've seen through Gloria's lies sooner."

Brittany let out a bitter laugh. "You think?"

"I know it doesn't make up for what happened," he continued, "but if you're willing, we'd like to have you back. Your position is still open."

Brittany hesitated, the anger in her chest warring with a flicker of relief. "I'll think about it," she said, her voice cool. She wasn't ready to forgive, but she wasn't about to let Gloria's poison rob her of her career either.

Reconnecting with her friends was harder. Weeks of Gloria's manipulation had left cracks in their trust, and while some of them had apologized, others stayed distant, unsure how to bridge the gap.

Kelly was the first to reach out, showing up at Brittany's door with a bottle of wine and a sheepish smile. "I fucked up," she admitted as soon as Brittany let her in. "I should've had your back."

Brittany studied her for a long moment before stepping aside. "Come in," she said finally. "We got a lot to talk about."

The conversation was raw and uncomfortable, but it was a start. By the end of the night, they were laughing over old memories, the weight of Gloria's betrayal beginning to lift.

Marcus showed up a few days later, standing awkwardly on her doorstep with a bouquet of daisies in hand. Brittany stared at him through the screen door, her arms crossed.

"What you doin' here, Marcus?" she asked, her tone cold.

"I came to apologize," he said, his voice low. "For not believin' you. For lettin' her get in my head. I was wrong, Britt. About everything."

Brittany didn't move, her heart twisting at the sincerity in his eyes. "You really let her come between us," she said, her voice trembling. "You were supposed to have my back."

"I know," he said, stepping closer. "And I hate myself for it. But I'm here now. If you'll let me, I wanna make it right."

She studied him for a long moment before opening the door. "You got a lot to prove," she said, her tone softer now. "But I'm willin' to let you try."

The days turned into weeks, and slowly, Brittany began to rebuild. Her apartment felt less like a prison and more like a sanctuary as she cleaned out the remnants of Gloria's presence. She replaced broken furniture, hung new curtains, and even painted the walls a fresh, vibrant color. It was a small step, but it felt like reclaiming her space, her life.

At work, she took her position back with a new sense of purpose. The whispers and side-eyes from her coworkers didn't bother her as much anymore. She had faced worse and survived. Her confidence grew with each passing day, her stride a little more sure, her voice a little louder.

One night, Marcus invited her to dinner, a quiet evening at his place. She hesitated but agreed, curious to see how far he was willing to go to mend their fractured relationship.

He had cooked her favorite fried chicken, mac and cheese, and collard greens. The effort made her smile, though she didn't let it show too much.

As they ate, he reached across the table, his hand brushing hers. "I know I let you down," he said softly. "But I'm not lettin' that happen again."

Brittany met his gaze, the walls around her heart softening just a little. "You got a lot to prove," she said, echoing her earlier words. "But I'm startin' to believe you mean it."

Gloria's trial was the final chapter of the nightmare. Brittany sat in the courtroom, her hands clenched in her lap as Gloria was led in, her once-confident demeanor replaced by a hollow, defeated expression. The evidence against her was damning testimonies from past victims, recorded conversations, and Brittany's own statement.

When the verdict was read guilty on all counts Brittany felt a weight lift from her chest. It wasn't joy or even satisfaction, but relief. Gloria's reign of terror was over.

That night, Brittany sat on her balcony, the city lights twinkling in the distance. Tanisha joined her, a bottle of champagne in hand.

"To new beginnings," Tanisha said, raising her glass.

Brittany clinked hers against it, a small smile playing on her lips. "To takin' my life back."

As she sipped her drink, Brittany felt a sense of peace she hadn't known in months. The scars Gloria had left would take time to heal, but for the first time, Brittany felt like she was in control. Her life was hers again, and she wasn't about to let anyone take it from her.

# Chapter 17: The Aftermath

Brittany sat on the edge of her bed, the glow of the morning sun creeping through the blinds. The weight of everything hung over her like a heavy chain, dragging her down even as she tried to rise above it. Gloria might have been behind bars, but her presence lingered, like a shadow that wouldn't let go.

The coffee table was cluttered with half-empty mugs and unopened mail. Brittany's phone buzzed, vibrating against the wood. She reached for it with a hesitant hand, her heart skipping a beat when she saw Tanisha's name.

"Yo, T," Brittany said, her voice hoarse from the restless night.

"Girl, go to Hood News and Happenins page on Instagram?" Tanisha's tone was urgent, laced with tension.

Brittany frowned. "Nah, what's goin' on?"

"They got posts talkin' 'bout Gloria. They pullin' out all kinds of shit on her."

Brittany's stomach twisted. "Like what?"

"Like how she done this before," Tanisha said. "Not just you, Britt. There's other people. One chick in Jersey, one in Ohio, Florida, another one in Philly. Same story she weasels her way in, destroys they lives, and bounces. And that's just the surface."

Brittany hung up and wen to the page, her hands shaking as she scrolled through the posts. When she landed on the post, Gloria's face filled the screen, her mugshot plastered next to footage of the courthouse steps. Photos where reporters buzzed around, microphones in hand, spouting details of her elaborate schemes.

"...accused of manipulating and sabotaging multiple victims across state lines..."

"...previous incidents dating back nearly a decade..."

"...described as a master manipulator with a dangerous obsession..."

The words blurred together, but Brittany couldn't look away. It was all there, laid out for the world to see. The calculated lies, the trail of destruction. And yet, hearing it from strangers didn't make it easier. It made it worse.

She sat the phone down. Gloria's past was horrifying, but it was the betrayal of her own friends that stung the most. They had doubted her, turned their backs when she needed them most. And even now, as some of them tried to make amends, Brittany couldn't shake the bitterness.

Later that day, Brittany decided to clear her mind with a walk. The city buzzed around her, alive with the sounds of car horns, distant laughter, and the occasional shout. It felt both familiar and alien, like she was out of sync with the world.

She stopped at a small café, ordering a coffee and sitting by the window. She watched people pass by, their lives moving forward while hers still felt stuck. Her mind wandered, flashes of Gloria's twisted smile creeping into her thoughts.

"Brittany?"

The voice startled her. She looked up to see Kelly standing by her table, holding a to-go cup. Her expression was hesitant, almost apologetic.

"Hey," Brittany said cautiously, her fingers tightening around her mug.

"Mind if I sit?" Kelly asked.

Brittany shrugged, nodding toward the empty seat. "Do what you want."

Kelly sat, fidgeting with the sleeve on her cup. "I heard about the trial," she said softly. "I just... I can't believe it. Everything she did. I feel so stupid for not seein' it."

Brittany took a sip of her coffee, letting the silence stretch between them. Finally, she said, "You believed her over me. All of y'all did."

"I know," Kelly said quickly. "And I'm sorry. I was wrong. We were all wrong. I just... I don't know how to fix this."

"Maybe you can't," Brittany said bluntly. "But I ain't got the energy to hold onto that shit anymore. I'm tryna move forward."

Kelly nodded, her eyes glistening. "If you ever need anything, I'm here. For real."

Brittany didn't respond, but the weight in her chest felt a little lighter as Kelly walked away.

That evening, Brittany sat in her living room, scrolling through her phone. The headlines about Gloria's trial were relentless, each one more damning than the last. She paused on a video clip, her thumb hovering over the play button before she finally gave in.

The footage showed Gloria in the courtroom, her demeanor icy and unrepentant. The prosecutor detailed her crimes with precision, painting a picture of a woman driven by envy and greed. As Brittany listened, a chill ran down her spine.

"...she targeted individuals she envied, systematically dismantling their lives to fulfill her delusions of superiority..."

The words hit Brittany like a punch. It wasn't just about her. Gloria had done this over and over, leaving behind a trail of shattered lives. And Brittany had almost been one of them.

The days passed, and while the trial continued to dominate the news and social medai, Brittany focused on reclaiming her life. She returned to work, her confidence slowly rebuilding with each project she completed. Her coworkers were cautious but supportive, their apologies tentative but sincere.

Marcus was a constant presence, his efforts to make amends unwavering. He showed up with dinner on the nights she worked late, listened without judgment when she vented, and reminded her of who she was before Gloria's shadow consumed her.

One evening, as they sat on the couch watching a movie, Marcus turned to her, his expression serious. "You know you're the strongest person I know, right?"

Brittany raised an eyebrow. "You just sayin' that 'cause you feel guilty."

"I mean it," he said, his voice firm. "You fought through all that shit she put you through. You didn't let her break you."

Brittany looked at him, her walls lowering just a little more. "She almost did," she admitted. "But I ain't lettin' her win."

On the day of Gloria's sentencing, Brittany debated whether to go to court. She didn't want to see Gloria again, didn't want to give her the satisfaction of knowing she still occupied space in her mind. But something in her needed closure.

The courtroom was packed, the tension palpable as the judge read the sentence: twenty-five years for fraud, harassment, attempted murder and a laundry list of other charges. Gloria's expression didn't change, her defiance unbroken even as the gavel slammed down.

Brittany watched from the back of the room, her emotions a whirlwind of relief, anger, and sadness. Gloria was gone, but the scars she'd left behind would take time to heal.

As Brittany walked out of the courthouse, the weight on her shoulders felt lighter. The city stretched out before her, bustling and alive, and for the first time in a long time, she felt like she could breathe.

That night, Brittany stood on her balcony, the cool breeze brushing against her skin. The lights of the city twinkled below, a reminder that life went on. She wasn't the same woman she had been months ago. She was stronger now, sharper, more resilient.

She raised her glass, toasting to the city, to herself, to survival. The road ahead wasn't easy, but it was hers to walk.

# Chapter 18: Back to Life

The city stretched out before Brittany, glittering with life under the dark canvas of the night. From her balcony, she could see everything the bustling streets, the glowing signs, the hum of a world that never truly slept. It was a view she'd always loved, a reminder of the life she'd fought to reclaim. But tonight, the view didn't bring her the peace it usually did.

The letter sat on the table behind her, its edges curling slightly from where she had crumpled it in her trembling hands. The words were burned into her mind, each one dripping with menace:

*"This ain't over. I'll be back."*

It had arrived earlier that afternoon, tucked between bills and flyers in her mailbox. At first, she'd thought it was a joke some cruel prank by someone who didn't understand what she'd been through. But the handwriting was unmistakable, the slanted scrawl as familiar as Gloria's twisted smirk.

The paper smelled faintly of prison sterile, cold, and faintly metallic. Brittany had read the letter over and over, each word tightening the knot in her stomach. Gloria hadn't just been defeated. She was waiting, plotting, and still holding onto her delusions of control.

Brittany paced her living room, the letter clenched in her fist. Tanisha's voice echoed through the speaker of her phone, sharp and concerned.

"She's in prison, Britt. She can't do nothin' to you now," Tanisha said, trying to sound confident, but Brittany could hear the unease in her tone.

"You don't get it, T," Brittany snapped. "Gloria don't let shit go. She's obsessed. She got nothin' but time in there to figure out how to come back."

"So what you gon' do?" Tanisha asked. "Move? Change your name? What?"

"I don't know," Brittany admitted, her voice cracking. "But I can't let her win. Not again."

That evening, Marcus came over, his face a mask of concern. Brittany handed him the letter without a word, watching as his jaw tightened with each line he read.

"This bitch really don't know when to quit," he muttered, tossing the letter onto the table. "She locked up, Britt. She ain't gon' touch you."

"You don't know that," Brittany said, her arms crossed over her chest. "She got people on the outside. What if she sends somebody?"

Marcus sighed, stepping closer to her. "You ain't gotta worry bout that shit, Britt. I'm here. We'll handle it, whatever it is."

Brittany searched his eyes, her own filled with a mix of fear and determination. "I just want my life back," she whispered. "For real this time."

"You got it back," Marcus said firmly. "Now you just gotta keep it."

The days that followed were a blur of tension and paranoia. Brittany found herself looking over her shoulder constantly, jumping at every unexpected sound. Her apartment, once a sanctuary, now felt like a cage.

She started changing her routines taking different routes to work, avoiding the places she and Gloria used to frequent. She even considered moving, but the thought of uprooting her life again felt like letting Gloria win.

At night, she slept with a knife under her pillow, her dreams haunted by Gloria's voice, her laugh, her eyes. She'd wake up in a cold sweat, the letter's words ringing in her ears: *"This ain't over."*

One evening, Brittany sat at her kitchen table, staring at the letter once more. She couldn't let it consume her. Gloria wanted her scared, wanted her to spiral. Brittany had to remind herself that Gloria's power was gone at least for now.

She picked up her phone and called her therapist, someone she hadn't spoken to in years. The conversation was awkward at first, but as Brittany began to open up, the weight on her chest started to lift.

"You've been through something traumatic," the therapist said. "It's natural to feel afraid. But fear is what Gloria thrives on. Don't give her that power."

Brittany nodded, even though the words felt easier said than done.

That night, Brittany stood on her balcony again, the city stretching out before her. The air was cool, the faint hum of life below a reminder that the world kept turning. She held a glass of wine in one hand, the other gripping the railing as she stared out into the night.

She thought about everything Gloria had taken from her her friends, her confidence, her sense of safety. But she also thought about what she'd gained. She was stronger now, sharper, more aware of who she was and what she could endure.

As the city lights flickered in the distance, Brittany made a silent vow to herself. She would not let Gloria or anyone else control her life again. The battle had been won, but she knew the war wasn't over. It might never be.

She raised her glass to the skyline, her voice steady as she whispered to the night, "Bring it on."

And with that, Brittany turned and walked back inside, ready to face whatever came next.

# Don't miss out!

Visit the website below and you can sign up to receive emails whenever Rachael Reed publishes a new book. There's no charge and no obligation.

https://books2read.com/r/B-A-WXARB-KBMLF

BOOKS 2 READ

Connecting independent readers to independent writers.

Did you love *Everybody That Grin Ain't Ya Friend*? Then you should read *Return to Sender*[1] by Rachael Reed!

## Return to Sender

Ain't nothin' more dangerous than a jealous heart. Lori and Karesha been tight since day one, but when love and loyalty get tested, everything falls apart. Karesha's life been hittin' bumps outta nowhere money problems, fights with her man Rob, and her world crumblin' piece by piece. What she don't know is her own best friend been pullin' the strings, usin' voodoo to twist the knife.

While Karesha prays for strength, leanin' on her faith and Rob to get through, Lori spirals deeper into her obsession, tryna destroy what she can't have. But every spell backfires, pushin' Karesha and Rob closer instead of tearin' them apart. As secrets start spillin', Lori snaps,

---

1. https://books2read.com/u/bPdE07

2. https://books2read.com/u/bPdE07

unleashin' a storm that shatters everything and puts Karesha's life on the line.

When the dust settles, who gon' be left standin'? **Return to Sender** is a dark, raw, and twisted tale where trust is broken and revenge always finds its way back.

# Also by Rachael Reed

**Sis**
Sis 2 Blood on the Streets

**Standalone**
Codefendant
Codefendant
Once a Cheater
Once a Cheater
Passport Bro
What Happens in Prison
Preference
Sprinkle Sprinkle
Championship Bad
Street Exodus
Street Exodus
Street Royalty
Pawns of Power
SIS
Cartel Bloodline
Get Money Girls
Skip the Games
Til Death Do Us Part

Backpage Hustle
Link in Bio
The Virgin and The Kingpin
A Gangsta's Heart
Boosters
Can't Turn a Hoe Into a Housewife
Better you Than Me
Wig Dealer: How to Start Your wig Business
Trail Ride Blues
Demure Diva
Queen of the Carnival
Caribbean Carnival Hoe
How to Glow Up! Make 2025 Your Best Year
How to Lose 10 Pounds in a Month
What is Project 2025? The Easy to Understand Guide
What Is A Tariff
Natural Hair Growth Oil with 50 Recipes
Regrow Hair Naturally in 3 Weeks
Hustlin Through the Holidays
Same Shit Different Year
Return to Sender
85 South
Everybody That Grin Ain't Ya Friend